GET ALL
WITH JUST ONE

$50 VALUE

◆ **Hotel Discounts**
up to 60%
at home
and abroad
◆ **Travel Service** -
Guaranteed lowest published
airfares plus 5% cash back on
tickets ◆ **$25 Travel Voucher**
◆ **Sensuous Petite Parfumerie**
collection ◆ **Insider**
Tips Letter with
sneak previews of
upcoming books

You'll get a FREE personal card, too.
It's your passport to all these benefits— and to
even more great gifts & benefits to come!

There's no club to join. No purchase commitment. No obligation.

HP-PP5A

Enrollment Form

☐ **Yes!** I WANT TO BE A *Privileged Woman.*
Enclosed is one *PAGES & PRIVILEGES*™ Proof of
Purchase from any Harlequin or Silhouette book currently for
sale in stores (Proofs of Purchase are found on the back pages
of books) and the store cash register receipt. Please enroll me
in *PAGES & PRIVILEGES*™. Send my Welcome Kit and FREE
Gifts — and activate my FREE benefits — immediately.

More great gifts and benefits to come.

NAME (please print)

ADDRESS   APT. NO

CITY   STATE   ZIP/POSTAL CODE

PROOF OF PURCHASE ONLY

**NO CLUB!
NO COMMITMENT!**
*Just one purchase brings
you great Free Gifts and
Benefits!*

Please allow 6-8 weeks for delivery. Quantities are limited. We reserve the right to
substitute items. Enroll before October 31, 1995 and receive one full year of benefits.

Name of store where this book was purchased_____

Date of purchase_____

Type of store:
  ☐ Bookstore   ☐ Supermarket   ☐ Drugstore
  ☐ Dept. or discount store (e.g. K-Mart or Walmart)
  ☐ Other (specify)_____

Which Harlequin or Silhouette series do you usually read?

_____

Complete and mail with one Proof of Purchase and store receipt to:
U.S.: *PAGES & PRIVILEGES*™, P.O. Box 1960, Danbury, CT 06813-1960
Canada: *PAGES & PRIVILEGES*™, 49-6A The Donway West, P.O. 813,
        North York, ON M3C 2E8

HP-PP5B

▼ DETACH HERE AND MAIL TODAY! ▼

"You're a man of no principles at all!"

Natasha ground out the words through clenched teeth. "You're vile!" she continued. "You only kissed me to humiliate me!"

"Have I succeeded?" Ruan queried mildly.

Natasha's mouth dropped open in pure amazement. "What? You admit...you cold-blooded, ruthless—" She was almost incoherent with rage. "This blatant act of revenge is unpardonable!" she cried.

"I was just doing a little research," Ruan stated with a low, sinister laugh.

Childhood in Portsmouth, England, meant grubby knees, flying pigtails and happiness for *SARA WOOD*. Poverty drove her from typist and seaside landlady to teacher, till writing finally gave her the freedom her Romany blood craved. Happily married, she has two handsome sons. Richard is married, calm, dependable, drives tankers; Simon is a roamer—silversmith, roofer, welder, always with beautiful girls. Sara lives in the Cornish countryside. Her glamorous writing life alternates with her passion for gardening, which allows her to be carefree and grubby again!

Books by Sara Wood

HARLEQUIN PRESENTS
1692—THE VENGEFUL GROOM
1715—SOUTHERN PASSIONS

Don't miss any of our special offers. Write to us at the following address for information on our newest releases.

Harlequin Reader Service
U.S.: 3010 Walden Ave., P.O. Box 1325, Buffalo, NY 14269
Canadian: P.O. Box 609, Fort Erie, Ont. L2A 5X3

SARA WOOD

Shades of Sin

Harlequin Books

TORONTO • NEW YORK • LONDON
AMSTERDAM • PARIS • SYDNEY • HAMBURG
STOCKHOLM • ATHENS • TOKYO • MILAN
MADRID • WARSAW • BUDAPEST • AUCKLAND

With my thanks to my favorite balloon pilot,
John we're-running-out-of-land Watkins, and
Shirley Rogers, beauty therapist at Plymouth's
Moat House.

ISBN 0-373-11765-5

SHADES OF SIN

First North American Publication 1995.

CHAPTER ONE

RUAN GARDINI slid the champagne into his flight bag and let his dark, secretive gaze wander up a pair of distractingly long legs, a thigh-freezing skirt and a shapely body, till it reached the sulky face of a stunning bottle-blonde.

'Of course I have to go,' he said curtly, in answer to her sullen question. 'Natasha needs keel-hauling.' A cruel smile disfigured his handsome Italian features. The thought was enjoyable. Slowly he straightened, testing his iron discipline by containing his impatience to be off.

'Natasha, Natasha!' complained Caroline irritably. 'You're obsessed with the woman——'

'No. With revenge,' he corrected drily. 'And I've only waited four years.'

'You? Wait? Action man himself?' queried Caroline in disbelief.

'Some things give a more intense pleasure if they're done properly,' he said, with a faintly mocking smile. 'A little preparation, a gradual build-up, slow and sweet, and the climax is more...profound. More extreme. Well worth the anticipation.'

She shivered at his ruthless analysis. 'The whole escapade seems dangerous to me,' she frowned. 'Full of pitfalls.'

'I can handle the flight,' Ruan drawled. 'The cross-winds are treacherous but I know what I'm doing.'

'I *meant* this Natasha,' snapped Caroline. 'If she's the two-faced bitch you say——'

'I can cope with anything that fate throws at me now.' He zipped up his black leather flying jacket over his naked chest. 'My parents were Sicilian,' he murmured, drawing on his leather gauntlets. 'That gives me a head start where a healthy spot of vengeance is concerned. And fortunately the greedy Natasha will do cartwheels for a fast buck and the prospect of milking a rich man.'

'She'll want *you*, then,' muttered Caroline.

'I do hope so,' said Ruan sardonically, fully aware that Caroline was a head-hunter of wealthy men too.

Noticing her sour look, he studied her dispassionately as if she were plain and sexless instead of oozing allure from every inch of her curvaceous body. She was getting a little possessive. He'd have to deal with that problem later.

He pushed back the unruly lock of raven hair that had fallen on to his forehead. The light of excitement at the prospect of danger made his eyes shimmer with an unholy brilliance. This would be his most hazardous landing yet and there was a good chance it wouldn't come off. His pulses raced and the energy inside him became impossible to contain.

'I'll contact you by radio only in an emergency,' he said with sudden staccato speed. 'You know what to do if I ditch.'

'Ruan——!' Caroline shut her mouth at his scowl. She'd been by his side long enough to know that it didn't do to stifle him.

'Sing nicely at my funeral if I drown,' he said with a faint smile. 'But don't hold on to my coat-tails,' he added softly. 'I made that clear at the beginning. I'm a man alone, with no one to worry or grieve for me. I like the freedom of that situation—and I mean to keep it that way.'

He turned in abrupt dismissal. Caroline watched him take off—smoothly, effortlessly, with the consummate and commanding skill he displayed in everything he did. And she wondered what had happened in Ruan Gardini's lone-wolf past to have made him so remorselessly single-minded and so utterly pitiless.

Natasha excitedly parked her car at the top of Penmellin's sandy cove, dumped her luggage by the cottage door and gazed heavenwards in pure delight. A scarlet hot-air balloon was drifting up Percuil Creek, following the river's sinuous bends like an airborne rowing-boat on an incoming tide.

'Hi there! Hello!' she cried happily.

Her yell, echoing across the water, was accompanied by a vigorous windmilling of her arms and caused a flock of startled oyster-catchers to take flight in a whirr of black and white. There was a blast of flame from the balloon's burners and the whole inside of the balloon lit up so that it glowed like a red ball in the sullen sky.

'Oh, gorgeous,' she sighed in pure contentment. '*Gorgeous*!'

She was home. At last she was home! Overjoyed, Natasha hugged herself and blissfully inhaled the intoxicating air—the mingled salt and river smells she'd missed for so long. The last few years, she mused, had been empty and lonely, filled with activity—but no meaning. And although she'd longed to return, even from the very moment she'd left, it had taken her all this time to find the inner toughness to face familiar sights again.

The Roseland peninsula had both drawn and repelled her, filled as it was with painful memories. The lanes where she and Ruan had wandered hand in hand. The wooded valleys where they'd picnicked . . .

Unseen by anyone, she wandered to touch the crumbling walls of the ancient lime-kiln on the edge of the beach. She smiled, seeing again Ruan's body glistening in the light of the bonfire they'd lit there after a midnight swim. And the ruined fish cellars behind her cottage had been their childhood den, a look-out for smugglers, a knight's stronghold.

'Ruan,' she whispered, aching with the desolation, the misery of knowing that a lifetime stretched ahead without him. He'd been her whole world; she'd given everything into his safe keeping: her childhood, her laughter, her teenage years, her trust and her love. No wonder it had taken all her will-power to forget him. No wonder she had found it hard to cope.

Her fingers lightly rested on the rough bark of the huge pine tree where she and Ruan had once played pirates—till he'd left for real-life piracy and the lure of easy gold and easier women.

Her face stilled, as the image came to her of Ruan's eyes flashing like sword-blades, his lacerating tongue destroying her future hopes, his deep contempt for her curling his sensual mouth till he seemed like a snarling animal, ready to rip her apart with his bare teeth.

'You can't hurt me any more!' she muttered defiantly, willing the ghastly memories back into hiding. 'I'm happy!'

Or was she? Her lower lip trembled and all her old vulnerability flowed back as if she'd never suppressed it with such meticulous, painstaking care.

She leant her head against the resinous trunk of the lone pine tree, slowly disciplining herself to forget the guilt she'd lived with for so long and had almost worked through her system. He'd deserved ruin. He had no morals at all and Roseland was well rid of him. Yet…she knew she'd never forget him—not his deceitful charm, his seductive liquid-sun voice or his explosive kisses.

Forget him? How could she forget the reason for her whole existence? Natasha groaned. Back ten minutes, and already her thoughts were full of the charlatan!

'Oh, rot in hell, Ruan Gardini, wherever you are!' she shouted angrily into the silence.

Her resentful gaze lifted to the balloon. Slowly, surely, its serenity and soaring freedom calmed her jangling nerves. For a while she watched, entranced by the magical sight, the long corn-silk strands of her hair blowing back from her face in the gentle breeze and making her look for all the world like a swimming mermaid. Then she turned to feast her eyes on her old home, allowing herself the rare luxury of sentiment.

The cob-stone cottage, squatting on the edge of the beach as it had for over two hundred years, seemed infinitely welcoming and enduring. Here, she could be herself—no longer an efficient, rather detached city girl running from intimacy, but someone who valued the love and warmth of trusted old friends. This was where she belonged. Home.

She sighed, realising ruefully that she should never have tried to be false to her nature. She'd hadn't liked the unemotional person she'd become; somehow, by the mere fact of removing Ruan from her heart, she'd destroyed her own compassion.

Gladly shedding layers of her sophisticated veneer with every step, she went to unlock the cottage door, eager to change. Figure-hugging pewter suits weren't exactly appropriate for remote Cornwall, she thought wryly.

'Look out belo-o-ow!'

The strangled cry stopped her dead. She whirled around and gasped in consternation because the balloon was hovering some fifty feet above the beach. It was too low to clear the trees in the narrow, steep-sided valley that ran down to the cove from Tredinnick House—and yet too high to land on the sandy shore.

'Oh, my God!' she whispered, rooted to the spot.

'I'm coming dow-w-wn!' came the pilot's bellow.

Before the appalled Natasha could respond, the balloon's fabric began to flap at the top and she knew for sure that something had gone terribly wrong. 'No!' she breathed in horror.

'Geronimo!' yelled the now invisible pilot, either inebriated or hysterical and no wonder: the balloon was plummeting like a stone, straight for the ground.

He'd be killed. Or dreadfully injured. 'I'm coming!' she screamed encouragingly, hitching up her slim skirt to her thighs in a flash and slipping off her high heels to race like the wind for the stretch of flat sand.

The base of the basket met the ground with a heavy crack of wicker and a loud groan of protest from the man presumably crouching inside. She reached the basket in two strides of her long legs—and was on the point of grabbing one of the rope handles when the whole thing toppled over on to its side. A 'whoosh' of fabric landed on her face, sprang into the air again and settled with a rustling sigh. Natasha found herself floundering on the ground beneath a sea of collapsed scarlet silk.

And a man. An inert male body sprawled across her. Leather-clad. Heavy. Her heart skipped a beat. Dead, was he dead?

'Help—mphhh!'

Her panic-stricken yell had been muffled by a mountain of softly drifting material and Natasha spluttered, working it from her mouth. The fabric flopped over her face and nostrils, suffocating the breath from her. In a frenzy of terror, she began to claw at it as it slid silkily over her face and hands like the sensual touch of a lover. Ruan, she thought crazily, quite illogically linking the two.

The man groaned. 'Mother,' he mumbled indistinctly, his face buried in her thick hair.

Not dead! Natasha's tense body relaxed with utter relief. Delirious, stunned, crazy or maybe rolling drunk, but living! 'You're alive!' she breathed into the blanketing fabric.

He moaned again and shifted his weight, bringing the smell of leather strongly to her nostrils. His hands, clad in heavy gauntlets, accidentally came into contact with her thighs and Natasha stiffened with automatic revulsion.

'Alive,' he agreed thickly. 'It's...not Mother,' he added, his hot breath warming a circle on her scalp.

Natasha smiled wryly to herself at the man's dazed wanderings and at last managed to elbow some of the material from her face so that she could speak clearly and push—ineffectually—at the massive shoulders. 'You're absolutely right,' she said, briskly, thinking this physical intimacy had gone on long enough. 'I'm glad I broke your fall, but you're heavy. Would you mind getting off me?'

'What luck you were there!' The pilot chuckled deep and low, his warm, moist breath shimmering over Natasha's throat and jaw as his head lifted away from her neck. Despite the still partly muffled voice, something in his tone and its deep timbre was alarmingly familiar. Impossible, she thought, her heart beginning to thud... 'But then, I always had the luck of the devil, didn't I?' the pilot added with a light irony—and total clarity.

She gasped, the shock running through her in a series of nauseating waves as the awful truth dawned and her heart raced crazily. Ruan! That was Ruan's arrogant laugh. Ruan's husky, all too masculine body, Ruan's firm hands confidently holding her waist on the pretext of lifting his weight from her a little. Eventually she found her voice to query the obvious.

'*Ruan?*' she rasped.

The pressure eased a bit more from her body and his dark, handsome face swam into view, demonic in the glimmering red light filtering through the crimson balloon. Natasha felt her whole being sag in dismay at her reaction to seeing him again. Her feelings hadn't been cauterised after all, only put into cold storage. She'd hoped never to meet him, never to feel this lurch of hopeless longing for a man who wasn't worth agonising over. But her heart's wound had opened already.

'Hello, Tasha,' he drawled sardonically, as if dropping out of the sky were the normal way to call on old friends. And enemies. 'Hello, Tasha's mouth.' His warm lips briefly touched hers before she could twist away and she tasted the salty tang of the sea. 'Welcome to *Scarlett*.'

She frowned. Somehow, apparently so completely confused by his sudden appearance, she'd failed to keep up with his train of thought. 'Scarlet what?' she asked irritably.

'It's the name of my balloon.' He gazed at her in cynical amusement as she tried to wriggle from beneath him and he pressed down with his legs which straddled her thighs, digging his toes into the sand to imprison her more securely. '*Scarlett*'s a rather flighty character in *Gone With the Wind*. She comes to earth with a bump after meeting a handsome, rakish ne'er-do-well——'

'I know the story,' she said coldly, glaring at him. 'I've met the rat who's his clone. Get off me.'

'Glad I don't have to explain the whole plot.' His mouth quirked. 'So. Fancy meeting you here.'

She tried to compose her bewildered mind and realised—a little late for modesty—that his chest had lowered again to press against her heaving breast which was rising and falling with every jerky breath she took. He'd be fully aware that she didn't feel as calm as she pretended, she thought with irritation. And his face, his sardonic, amused face, had come to within an inch or so of hers, as if they were still lovers embracing on the beach one starlit night.

'Remove your body,' she grated, biting out each word. 'It's landed on private property.'

'Oh? Thought I was on common ground,' he murmured insolently. But he put his hands back as if to do as she asked and his gauntlets slid almost—but not quite accidentally, she thought angrily, along the side of her nylon-clad thigh. 'Interesting!' he whispered huskily.

The awe in his voice dried her throat and all she could do was to mouth her protests like a gasping fish. She felt her body jerk spasmodically. Because, as if unable to accept what his gloved hand was telling him, he was checking with deliberate, tantalising thoroughness that almost the whole length of each of her legs *was* uncovered—and apparently inviting his touch.

'Ruan! Please...!' croaked Natasha. She felt mortified. Her pelvic muscles had contracted in an involuntary reaction to the undeniably erotic touch of satiny leather on silken thigh. His fingers moved higher and she held her breath, speechless, only her huge clouded eyes indicating her alarm.

'Saints preserve us!' he marvelled, his voice husky with masculine appreciation. 'That's what I call a short skirt!'

Natasha tightened her muscles against the onslaught of sensations that were threatening her firmly repressed sexuality. Wonderfully supple, smooth gauntleted hands skimmed over the soft, giving flesh above her suspenders.

Ruan's compelling green eyes seemed dark with desire, his mouth softened and irresistibly inviting. She felt all her senses stir and inhaled with a guilty pleasure the gentle, rapid breath that warmed her face, the long-forgotten maleness of him.

So tempting. Her eyes closed in despair at her weakness for him because she knew full well what a terrible womaniser he was. She'd adored him since she could walk, idolised him with innocent reverence, loved him with a passion that had made her a part of him—— Till she'd discovered the dark side of his character and his evil secrets had weighted her love with a ton of cement and thrown it overboard.

And now she was back in his arms and he was looking at her as if he found her wildly exciting.

Natasha knew that to save her soul she had to dredge up the pain of his betrayal, not those balmy nights beside the creek, kissing under overhanging willow trees, or curling up in his rowing-boat and watching the stars move slowly in the heavens. With a disgraceful reluctance, she gritted her teeth and grabbed his boldly roaming hand in hers—which he brought to his lips and solemnly began to kiss, knuckle by knuckle, joint by joint, finger by finger...

Calm. Stay calm, she told herself fiercely, quelling the insurrection inside her of every hormone she'd ever produced. 'Ruan! Stop that!' The kisses ceased abruptly. Natasha recognised her twinge of disappointment, to her shame. 'What *ever* are you doing *here*?' she husked, cursing him resentfully for pitching her back into her nightmare past.

'Same as you. Taking advantage of our surprise reunion,' he said laconically. 'And trying to get my breath back.' He laughed softly. 'Like you. Been a lovely day, hasn't it?'

They'd parted enemies, hurling insults at one another, exploding with pent-up rage and bitterness, and a painful discovery on her part that gods could have feet of clay. And now he was making conversation! She ground her teeth in anger.

'Your sheer effrontery is breathtaking!' she said coldly.

'So I gather. But then it gets me places other men only dream of,' he murmured.

'I can imagine,' she muttered, thinning her mouth. Glaring up at him, she lay tense and stiff beneath the virile, leather-encased body which seemed intent, she thought nervously, on re-discovering her through pelvic contact alone.

'Hell of a landing, wasn't it?' he remarked smugly.

'It looked like a bodge-up to me,' she told him sarcastically. 'What are you doing here?' she repeated. 'I thought you'd gone from Penmellin for good. Or rather bad.'

'Miaow,' he drawled, and she flushed, annoyed that he'd driven her to make a catty remark. 'I've been enjoying myself in Africa, tying women up, giving them a few thrills,' he explained lazily, engrossed in pushing back wisps of her hair from her temples.

Disgust showed plainly on her pinched, pale face. 'Keep the vile secrets of your bedroom to yourself,' she snapped.

'Don't jump to conclusions,' he said softly. 'It's a bad habit of yours. I was tying them into life-jackets.'

'You find that thrilling?' she scorned.

He raised a sardonic eyebrow, kissing her with a light affection that infuriated her with its insincerity. 'How innocent you are!' he mocked. 'Touch can be infinitely exciting between people who are attracted physically to each other. Though I must admit the thrill factor increased when we all got on the rafts and hurtled down the white-water rapids of the Zambesi. But that was last week. You know me. I can't settle anywhere for long. I get bored and move on.'

'Like a disease,' she said, opting for sarcasm to cover the irrational shaft of jealousy.

'Sounds like me,' he agreed. 'An affliction—perhaps accompanied by a fever—that's irresistible, unavoidable, potentially fatal. Deadly.' He loomed over her menacingly. 'So here I am to plague you,' he murmured in his soft, throaty voice, 'back for new delights, new women to infect, different thrills.'

A dreadful suspicion formed in her mind. Perhaps she might be put on his hit list. 'Luckily for me, one nasty dose has made me immune,' she said baldly. 'And you'll find no excitement here.'

'I disagree. It's been pretty thrilling so far,' he contradicted. 'And if the action flags, well, I'm an expert at making things happen.'

'I'm getting claustrophobia,' she muttered, desperately quelling the peril she felt herself in, lying there, trapped beneath him... And miles from human habitation. 'If you're the expert, make my escape happen!' she frowned, her grey-blue eyes soft with anxiety.

Ruan was unaffected by her plight. 'But it's beautifully dark, hot and intimate under here,' he murmured huskily, his unfairly sensual mouth virtually seducing her mind on its own.

'So,' she said pointedly, keeping her voice remarkably steady, 'is hell.' Her eyes had frozen to a remote ice-blue.

'And we're both in it together,' he said with soft menace. 'Want to join me, stoking the fire?'

Beneath the red canopy he smiled slowly, speculatively, and Natasha trembled, knowing how much he loved a challenge. Never once had he refused one, however crazy it had seemed. Her expression became apprehensive. Even when he failed he doggedly tried again and again, his arrogant Sicilian pride driving him to succeed. If she wanted hell, he'd give it to her in his own inimitable way.

'Why are you persisting in flirting with me?' she asked irritably. 'You don't care about me——'

'No, I don't,' he admitted laconically—too quickly for Natasha's pride.

'Then you can stop kissing me,' she said heatedly, 'and mauling me around!'

He smiled at her flushed, indignant face. 'Well, the icy reception's been coaxed away,' he said smugly. 'It seems I've tapped that well of passion inside you again. I like kissing women. What else does one do with them?'

'I can't believe that I was ever stupid enough to admire you,' she seethed. 'You're so *basic*. David was right—you're only aware of the physical world. The mind and the emotions are closed books to you. Now, how do I escape your gruesome clutches?'

The hard glitter in his eyes warned her of dangers to come. 'Only by being as pure as the angels,' he said softly.

'I am!' she protested grimly. 'I always have been.'

'Let's see,' he growled.

In panic, her hands wrestled with the silk, with the gorgeous sensation of the leather moulding his body, and with the strong masculine hands which had linked with hers above her head in playful victory. But the fierce, possessive kiss that crushed her lips and sent her mind into oblivion wasn't playful. It was total war—on her senses, her emotions, her cool, unruffled detachment.

He was getting to her again, almost without effort, and she recognised that fact with a despairing fury that gave her the strength to resist him. She tore her mouth away in outrage, blazing mad with herself.

'You *animal*! How dare you assault me? It's a pity the rapids didn't shoot *you*!' she raged.

'I'm a survivor,' he drawled. 'Of rapids, danger and women. I come out on top—like now.' The corners of his mouth twitched. 'Landing on a luxuriously padded female is quite a novelty. Obliging of you to fall at my feet.'

'Fall at . . . ! *Padded*?' Her breasts rose with the insult. 'This is all me!'

'I know,' he grinned wickedly. 'I felt.'

The blush suffused her face with scarlet. 'You—you . . . !' she spluttered.

His mouth claimed hers again. It seemed that she submerged and sank, floating beneath his hard, demanding body, miserably aware that there was a humiliating lick of life-giving fire sheeting through her that she only ever felt when Ruan kissed her.

'Someone's ringing bells,' whispered Ruan huskily.

Bells? All she could hear was the roaring in her ears. And since when did Ruan hear bells when he kissed women? 'The bell rings when it's the end of playtime,' she said in glacial tones.

'So it does. Ready for your next lesson?' he murmured.

She detected an edge of sinister determination in his words. As if... as if he was intending to be the one teaching her. 'What do you mean?' she asked cautiously, gazing into the dark eyes which sparkled with secret amusement.

He smirked. 'To begin with, you could do with a bit of tuition in kissing,' he said insolently.

'I'm getting it elsewhere,' she snapped in haughty defiance, pleased that his eyes narrowed speculatively, as if her answer had caused him to rehash his plans. Plans. She quailed at the thought. What might they be?

'Really? He's not very expert. Could your teacher be... David?' he asked with lazy curiosity.

She blinked at the suggestion. David? The idea was ludicrous! She'd come back to work in David's new health and beauty clinic, not to turn their childhood friendship into something deeper. David! If only she did love him—it would make life simple for once.

'Why do you say that?' she asked.

'Oh, I saw some luggage when I looked down. It seemed as if you're here to stay and I linked that with the fact that David has probably been pestering you to come back for years.'

'Well, yes, but——' she began, wincing at the tightening of his fingers as they dug into her arms. 'You're hurting!' she complained.

'Why didn't you come back before?' he asked softly.

Natasha stared in consternation. She couldn't answer that truthfully. She couldn't say it was because every darn blade of grass, every reed-bed and beach, every path and hedge all held memories of him, were all bound up in the details of delight and close affection they'd shared. She couldn't say that the sight of Roseland would have made her cry.

'My career——' she began huskily.

'It was more important than Roseland? Than Penmellin itself?' he suggested, his eyes threatening to tear her secrets from her.

She sought refuge in detachment, blindly reaching for her icy London mask which had long protected her emotions. 'This place has its limitations. No one ever made a fortune down here.'

'That's what you want, a fortune?' he asked carefully.

'Doesn't everyone?' she answered haughtily. 'Money can buy security,' she continued in a hard tone, thinking how she'd realised she'd never marry and would need to be totally independent. 'My ambition was to become successful.' She decided to elaborate and to suggest that she'd got over Ruan's hold on her emotions. 'And to have some fun and meet more sophisticated men——'

'Fun city. Sex, lies and videotape,' he murmured cynically. 'Then why the hell are you back here with unsophisticated David?'

Just in time, she remembered that David had asked her to keep his venture a secret until the beauty franchise had been granted. 'He made me an offer I couldn't resist,' she said casually.

'Did he, now?' His head turned slightly in an attitude of listening. 'I wonder if that's another pupil for me?' he drawled, silkily pleased.

Above the loud thudding of her heart, she suddenly heard the car approaching along the narrow, bumpy lane and she let out a long gasp of relief that they would no longer be alone. The car screeched to a halt by the cottage with a crunch of tyres. A door slammed and then came the sound of running feet.

'Anyone under there?' came David's yell.

Delighted at the surprise, Natasha threw Ruan a look of triumph. David would rescue her—as he had before, from Ruan's unwelcome attentions. 'The cavalry's arrived,' she said, pleased.

'But the action's here,' Ruan murmured.

Alerted by his unnervingly sensual tone, she opened her mouth to shout. Ruan ruthlessly took advantage of the opportunity and before she knew what was happening his tongue had slid between her lips and the warmth of him was flowing sweetly through her, melting every inch, every nook and cranny in her body, into a yearning submission.

In the darkness, beneath the canopy of silk, she lifted her hands in a helpless gesture and they drifted of their own volition to Ruan's thick black hair, revelling in the clean silky feel of the strands as his unruly waves slid through her fingers.

It had been such a long time since she'd been touched like this, kissed like this...with such intense fervour, such a depth of passion that every part of her was affected. Ruan's murmurs were vibrating throughout her body, filling her with a sense of sin. He was corrupting her; for his own amusement, he was driving her to share all the shades of sin he'd ever experienced.

Innocent, sexually vulnerable to erotic skills, she was apparently easily susceptible to a man as practised as Ruan. And she couldn't bear it—neither the sweet poignancy of the situation nor the sheer delight his attentions aroused. A moan of helpless despair sounded in her throat and he responded with a deep growl, making her limbs tremble with its raw, primitive savagery.

'Hello?' called David uncertainly, not unnaturally puzzled by the movement beneath the scarlet fabric. 'Anyone hurt? Need help?'

Me, she thought hysterically, sharp longing radiating through her from the erotic caress of Ruan's tongue on her protesting lips. He chuckled with male triumph and she froze in sudden realisation.

'This is deliberate, isn't it?' she seethed, ignoring David's hesitant calling. 'You're trying to annoy him because you found me in his arms four years ago!'

'You don't think I've been kissing you today for my *own* pleasure, do you?' he drawled, and then gave a low chuckle. 'What do you think David makes of our writhings?'

She could hardly speak for fury. 'My God, Ruan!' she ground out through her teeth. 'You're vile! You only kissed me to humiliate me!' she cried, appalled at his deception.

'Have I succeeded?' he queried mildly.

Her mouth dropped open in pure amazement. '*What*? You admit... You cold-blooded, ruthless—— *Oh*! I could almost excuse you if—if you'd been driven by passion!' she raged almost incoherently. 'But this—this blatant act of revenge is unpardonable! You foul, calculating swine! You rat-fink!'

'I was doing a little research,' he murmured, quite unfazed by her accusations. 'So much for the sophisticated men you've been dating. I'm fascinated to discover that you've learnt nothing more of the sensual arts since we were lovers and David kept hanging around, playing gooseberry.'

'I seem to remember you were the gooseberry last time,' she grated, and caught a blaze of real anger in Ruan's eyes. Maliciously glad to have reached a raw nerve, she raised her voice and yelled, 'David! It's me! Natasha!' She yanked her wrists from Ruan's crushing grip and thrashed around in frustration at the billowing scarlet above her. 'Get me out of this stuff!'

'Natasha? My God! What are you *doing* under there?' David cried.

Ruan gave a low, sinister laugh that made Natasha shiver with apprehension. 'The man's a fool.' He turned to bellow in David's direction. 'Where's your imagination, David?'

'Ohh! You're impossible!' she stormed in the stunned silence, while David processed the fact that she was with Ruan. Her fingers grabbed at the dark sweep of his hair and tightened, jerking his head up with a suddenness that somehow brought Ruan's vulnerable throat into contact with her sensitised mouth. Briefly she felt her lips travel over the flawless warm skin and knew that they had lingered to savour the sensation for a fraction too long. All the pulses in her body seemed to be throbbing like jungle drums. She blushed with the message they were sending her brain.

'Very sexy. Do that again,' he growled encouragingly.

Natasha glared. 'I'm tempted to bite through your jugular!' she said vehemently. 'Get *off*!' Her eyes blazed in fury, as there came the sound of David frantically trying to drag the material away from their entangled bodies.

'Leave it, David!' shouted Ruan. 'You'll rip the envelope! Curb your impatience! We're just coming.'

He reached up past her head, searching for something, his expression one of deep concentration. His lowered black lashes and the slide of his velvety cheek against hers flung all her emotions into chaos and she began to tremble.

'What are you doing?' she breathed warily, her mouth in a sulky pout of exasperation.

'I'm being tempted,' he said sardonically. 'By a mermaid with hair of spun gold that's flowing over the sand like a rippling river.'

'Keep your poetry and your lies for those who are stupid enough to believe them,' she grated harshly.

'Lies?' His face became serious as he contemplated her. 'Oh, no, Natasha; I am genuinely pleased to see you. I've waited for this moment for a long, long time.' His hands caressed her face, cupping it in a tender gesture that sent her heart racing. His smile was appealing and she mistrusted it instantly. 'This is cause for celebration. Two old friends meeting. I want to drink your health. There's some champagne in my flight bag. We'll catch up on news——'

'Champagne?' she scorned. 'You always did have big ideas. A flask of nourishing soup would have been more sensible.'

'But infinitely dull,' he argued in amusement.

'Don't you do *anything* like normal men?' she frowned.

'Like clean the car, mow the lawn, watch TV?' He shrugged. 'Some men get their kicks doing those things; I need something a little more exciting,' he said softly. He grinned disarmingly, dazzling her with the high-octane energy that fuelled his reckless drive through life. 'I get a high from danger,' he whispered huskily. 'That and women are the most exhilarating aphrodisiacs in the world. I'm helplessly addicted to both. I can never get all I need. So...' His mouth found hers again, crushing hard enough to obliterate all rational thought.

She felt him reach up to tug sharply at something and then cool air blew on her forehead as if they were exposed to the elements. But before she could wriggle from the clinch she became aware of David's loudly indignant gasp.

'Natasha! How could you?' he cried, in the tones of a scolding aunt.

'Oh, no!' she groaned, shutting her eyes tightly in embarrassment.

'That's a poor greeting for an old friend,' mocked Ruan.

Her stormy eyes flicked open as he eased his body from hers and stood up. He towered over her, big and menacing, his legs unnervingly male in the tightly moulded black leathers. She swallowed and forced her fingers to stay put and not respond to the irrational impulse to stroke the black satiny cloth which clung like a second skin to his muscular thighs. Ruan's thickly lashed eyes kindled as if he knew her dilemma. In a swift, lithe movement, he bent and his hands clamped around her waist, lifting her smoothly to her feet.

'With one bound, she was free. Or . . . she thought she was,' he murmured meaningfully, jerking her arrogantly into his body.

Not quite understanding how they'd surfaced so easily, she pulled back from Ruan as far as she could, arching her supple spine, nervous of the strength of his hands encircling her narrow waist. Around them in the gathering dusk, like a blood-red sea, lay the rippled balloon, and at one edge of the voluminous material stood the irate David with the porch oil lamp in his hand which spilled golden light on to Ruan's sardonic face.

'How—how did we——?'

'It's quite simple,' he said patronisingly. 'There's a piece of material sewn into the top of the balloon called the parachute. By collapsing it at a safe height, it's possible to make the basket drop straight to the ground. And we've just crawled out of that part rather like lugworms emerging from a hole.'

Her venomous eyes bored into his. 'You're the worm!' she muttered. 'If you're actually claiming that you could have got me out long ago, then why didn't you?'

'Please!' he drawled. 'Credit me with a little deviousness.'

'Oh, I do, I certainly do!' Life was nothing but an amusing diversion to Ruan, she reflected bitterly. 'You play with women like an angler playing a fish,' she muttered. 'And you don't care how deeply you hurt them before you throw them back.'

'They don't have to take my bait,' Ruan retorted, silky smooth. 'But they always do. Is that greed, do you think?' Natasha blushed bright scarlet. 'Yes, greed,' he said softly.

'You bastard! You took advantage of her!' accused David belligerently.

Ruan nodded, his expression cynical. 'Yes. Of course. I've always enjoyed kissing beautiful women. Or so my reputation would suggest. Didn't you tell Natasha once that I'd kissed more women than you'd had hot dinners? Of course, it was the kind of unoriginal remark I'd expect from you.'

She stared at him, dumb-struck with fury, her insides wrenching at the painful memory of David's gentle, tentative warning that he feared Ruan was seeing other women.

'I can't bear to think of your foul, lying mouth on hers!' hissed David angrily.

Natasha heard the bitterness in David's voice and her heart immediately went out to him. She knew that he'd always been sweet on her. 'Neither can I! It makes me feel sick!' she grated, hardly able to credit the fact that she hadn't fought tooth and nail to get away from Ruan. It was the web of sensuality he'd woven around her, she thought, excusing herself. 'You're a man of no principles at all, Ruan Gardini!' she snapped.

'That seems to sum up the general impression of me around here.' He leant towards her confidentially. 'I'd pull your skirt down now, if I were you,' he suggested in a conspiratorial whisper.

'Oh!' she cried, appalled. 'Why didn't you remind me?'

'You want an answer to that question?' Ruan murmured sardonically, staring at her shapely legs and thighs with a voracious hunger, his mouth incredibly carnal as she frantically tried to work the stubborn skirt down into place again with shaking, virtually useless fingers. David looked too shocked to speak.

She was almost weeping with embarrassment and self-reproach. '*No*! I don't!' She glanced guiltily at David again. 'He didn't do this, David—*I* did! I mean——!' Flustered, she gave the amused Ruan a look of loathing.

'Try to explain,' he said with completely insincere encouragement. 'He might be stupid enough to believe you. Personally, I wouldn't.'

'David,' she said distractedly, 'I saw the balloon was going to crash and I hitched my skirt up so I could run to the aid of the pilot. If I'd known it was *him*,' she added darkly, 'I'd have gone indoors and cheered myself hoarse while he broke his darn neck.'

'At last I'm getting a glimpse of the real Natasha,' remarked Ruan thoughtfully, his eyes hard as black granite. 'You're a heartless bitch really, aren't you? I'm surprised you let me make mad, passionate love to you just now——'

'You liar! We didn't!' she stormed, her eyes bright with angry tears. 'It's untrue and you know it!'

'By God, Ruan, if you've . . . ! Dammit, it's happened again; you've pushed your way into my life again, interfering . . . ! Leave Natasha alone! I could throttle you!' yelled David, losing his temper.

'No, David. You couldn't,' said Ruan calmly, his eyes lethal. 'Not in a month of Sundays.'

Suddenly she wanted to run, to get away from Ruan and his menacing sexuality, to escape the threat to the stable life she'd planned for herself. He was ruining her return, she thought miserably. It had been utterly magical before he'd turned up.

'I've had enough of this!' Tense and close to screaming, she made to walk across the expanse of crumpled scarlet but Ruan stopped her by quickly throwing his arm around her waist and dragging her back.

'No,' he murmured into her small, excruciatingly sensitised ear. 'Under, not over. I'll direct you.'

Her rebellious eyes slanted to his. 'Like hell you will!'

'Sure. Like hell I will,' he agreed enigmatically. 'We both know that's where I am and where I'm taking you. To hell.'

'What—what do you mean?' she breathed, a chill icing the bones of her spine. Ruan had a terrible sense of justice. Perhaps he had kissed her with such brutal disregard for her dignity because he wanted to hurt her for rejecting him. Well, she had news for him. She'd been in hell and was just clawing her way out and nothing would drag her back again.

'Isn't it hell being with me? Looking into my lying eyes? Feeling my deceitful mouth on yours, discovering that despite everything you know about me the flame still burns?' he asked quietly.

'Yes. It is,' she answered hoarsely, her pulses leaping in erratic little lurches. 'But——'

'Unfortunately you'll have to suffer my presence a little longer,' he murmured. 'Because if you walk across the envelope of my balloon you'll regret it. You're looking at one hundred and twenty feet of material so expensive that it would cost you all the luxuries you possess to pay for it.' A wintry smile passed fleetingly over his mobile mouth. 'I'd *love* to deprive you of your hard-earned cash. Go on, walk on it,' he challenged maliciously. 'I'll sue the clothes off your back.'

She bit her lip, hesitating. Whatever she did would give him satisfaction. The envelope didn't look as if it would be torn easily, but she didn't dare risk an expensive lawsuit. He might well claim damage even if there wasn't any.

'Ruan! Get Natasha over here immediately!' ordered the furious David.

'With pleasure. Stay there, my old friend. Natasha is about to impersonate a snake in the grass.' His mouth twitching at her exasperated intake of breath, Ruan balanced on one leg, unlacing his leather boots. He straightened, smiled mockingly at her and lobbed the boots in David's direction—none too carefully. 'Catch!' he urged, a fraction too late. David ducked, cursed, and began to forage around in the bushes for the boots.

Natasha gave Ruan a scathing look. 'You and I know perfectly well that you're able to throw a cricket ball several hundred yards and brain any beetle of your choice,' she said tightly. 'You *meant* to make David look inept.' Her mouth curled in scorn. 'How unpleasant can you get?'

'Hang around a while. You'll find out.' His glinting black eyes backed up the sinister edge to his voice. 'David asks for everything that comes to him. Everything,' he said silkily, picking up his flight bag. When he straightened, his face was bland and unreadable again. 'Besides, while we crawl along like a couple of undulating Dover soles, we need to keep the spectators occupied. Down, woman.' He pulled her relentlessly to her knees and held her fast, and it was plain that he was enjoying himself hugely.

'You're despicable,' she muttered.

'Perhaps we all are,' he said quietly. Then he lifted his eyebrow and the brief flash of pain she'd seen had gone, and she knew it must have been a trick of the light. 'This is more exciting than cleaning your car or watching TV, don't you think?' he queried. 'Come on, Tash. Enemy in sight,' he drawled. 'Dive, dive, dive.'

More than willing to get away from his sarcasm, she wriggled beneath the rustling material, muttering under her breath at Ruan's seductive manner, his unorthodox arrival and his infuriating command of the situation—And promised herself she wouldn't let him get under her defences again. She'd spent too long carefully expunging his reckless, devil-may-care image from her heart and her life, closing down all feeling to operate on a safer, more humdrum level.

She didn't want to feel vulnerable. She'd worked too hard for her armour. Here, in the safety of Penmellin, she'd expected to shed the steel skin she'd protected herself with. But Ruan was making her reinforce it. Because a disturbing truth persisted in worrying her. Infuriating though he was, Ruan made her feel *alive*.

He was chuckling behind her, probably at her neatly swaying rear end. She frowned, but part of her unaccountably wanted to giggle at the zany situation. She couldn't deny that. All her fiercely suppressed mischief bubbled inside her, restrained for so long, buried under bitter memories and the effort of holding back all her feelings. Now it seemed to be longing to be let out again.

Ruan caught her up and shuffled alongside her in an amiable way but Natasha knew there was nothing amiable about him in reality; he was as good-natured as a great white shark with hunger pangs.

She gritted her teeth. This was one shark who'd go hungry.

CHAPTER TWO

EVERYONE had noticed Natasha's adoration of Ruan and had warned her against him from the beginning; the lawless, fearless Ruan, worrying his adoring mother sick because he craved excitement as his peers craved potato fries and video games.

Even as a small boy he'd run wild, she remembered. Indifferent to authority and punishment, he'd played hookey from school, roaming the Roseland peninsula and turning up days later, dirty, hungry, his second-hand clothes torn, his hand-me-down shoes ripped to ribbons. Where he'd been, what he'd done, he'd never said, but the elation and zest for life that filled his whole body at those times had been utterly spellbinding.

She knew that he'd scaled the sheer Stack Rock, explored the honeycomb of flooded caves near by and often lived rough for days. Poor he might be, but not in courage or daring. And money and better breeding mattered nothing when he was around. He could charm anyone he chose. Women in particular, she thought bitterly. Moths to a flame. They'd all been burnt and had learned a hard lesson. Ruan single-mindedly pursued the pleasures of life and to hell with anyone's feelings.

'Natasha, remember the cellars at Tredinnick?' he asked, breaking into her thoughts.

She found that she'd stopped in her tracks. Disconcerted, she continued to crawl along grimly, easing herself handful by handful under the slippery envelope, reluctant to remember the idyllic days they'd spent in the huge, deserted house up the valley from Penmellin. 'No,' she lied grimly.

'Let me refresh your memory,' he murmured. 'Seven years old, thick braids bleached by the sun, blue-spotted shorts, white T-shirt, scared of the dark. But you trusted me and we ended up sitting on the cellar floor in the pitch blackness, eating a bag of pears I'd scrumped from the garden and telling each other of our ambitions.'

'Why remind me of my childish stupidity?' she snapped, the cherished image of his warm hand in hers and his proud hug of admiration too distressing to bear. Or the fact that he'd sworn solemnly to make a fortune and marry her. She blushed at her blind belief in him. 'You took advantage of me then as you did just now. All you wanted was someone to impress. I'm not proud that I ran around at your beck and call like an obedient dog.'

'It's amusing to reminisce sometimes,' he said softly. 'It shows us how far we've come since our childhood.'

Had she? she wondered. Even now, being close to him like this, she felt embraced by his powerful personality, almost swamped by the extraordinary sensations that played tunes on her nerves every time he came near.

Brought up in a colourless, loveless home by a widowed mother who'd been unable to show affection, she had been drawn helplessly to the notorious, self-sufficient Ruan and his boundless enjoyment of life. No one else had his magic. She sighed heavily.

'Water under the bridge,' she said lamely. Her legs began to tremble and she paused, incapable of going on for a moment.

'God, Tasha! There's the most wonderful curve to your back...' His questing hand swept its length. 'I'd advise you not to stay in that erotic position,' he said, his voice thickening to a slow cream.

'I don't have much choice,' she said grimly. 'You made me crawl under this darn thing.'

He gave a low laugh. 'There's always a choice—between one evil and another. The choices you make say

a great deal about your character. For instance, you preferred to risk being mauled by me, rather than risking
your bank balance.'

'I'm not enjoying this one little bit. But losing money
would have more of a lasting effect on me,' she snapped.

'Now that's an interesting interpretation,' he mused.
'We must see if it's true later.' To Natasha's infinite relief,
they emerged at last and Ruan sprang up lithely. 'And
here's my one-time rival David!'

He clapped enthusiastic hands on his old friend's
shoulders and David's knees buckled slightly beneath the
impact.

'Marvellous to see you after all this time, Natasha,'
said David, pointedly ignoring Ruan's hearty greeting.
He helped her up and warmly embraced her.

To her surprise, she felt an overwhelming urge to
remove herself from his arms, but perversely wanted to
annoy Ruan more. 'Hello,' she smiled. 'It's good to be
home.'

David's mouth moved briefly over hers, hesitated, then
pressed more firmly when she made no objection. She
instantly compared his kiss with Ruan's. There was no
comparison, she thought bleakly, either in technique or
result. Nothing tingled. Nothing glowed.

'You're a day early,' said David warmly, his hot breath
rather unpleasant on her face and making her recoil a
fraction. 'I'm so glad.'

'I couldn't wait,' she explained brightly.

'Finding it harder than you thought?' murmured
Ruan.

Her mouth thinned. His hawk-like eyes had detected
her dislike of physical contact with David. On impulse,
she decided she wouldn't explain why she'd come early.
She'd wanted to spend a day in her cottage all alone, in
the peaceful isolation of Penmellin Cove, but something
told her that Ruan would be irritated if he thought she'd
come purely because of David. And she wanted to shake

Ruan's complacency with a vehement malice that worried her.

'I simply couldn't wait,' she repeated softly. Her delicate, gentle face tipped up to David's appealingly. 'How lovely to see you.'

'This is terrific, Natasha,' he said, huskily. 'You know, I can't believe you're really coming to live with me.'

It seemed she was sensitive to every move Ruan made, because she knew he had imperceptibly tensed every muscle. It gave her some satisfaction that her remarks had had some effect, yet she didn't want to give David false hopes; she felt too sentimentally attached to him as a friend to hurt him. He'd been so good to her, so kind.

'You're paying enough for the privilege,' she said, forcing a light laugh to put the relationship on its proper commercial footing.

'Ah. The chink of gold. He's lured you here with the promise of riches,' drawled Ruan. 'This was the tempting offer?' he enquired, his voice ice-cold. The oil lamp on the ground cast sinister shadows on his face, and she detected in the shrewd darkness of his eyes the rapid working of his brain. 'David has offered you money to live with him and warm his bed?'

'How dare you?' yelled Natasha, aghast at his nerve.

'It's obvious he'd never get you any other way,' Ruan said with deliberate insolence.

She recoiled from his icy contempt. He was dangerous, always had been, and never more so than at this moment when he thought David had acquired something he considered his property, to keep or to discard at will.

'Wouldn't he?' she said haughtily.

'What the devil are you doing here?' asked David sourly.

'Can't you guess?' mocked Ruan, his sardonic smile broadening with David's increasing nervousness. Natasha watched the two men with some curiosity—one defensive and wary, the other confident and urbane. 'I'll let you into a secret,' Ruan said confidingly. 'Tredinnick was my declared goal.'

'Tre-Tredinnick?' David went white. 'Your...goal?'

Natasha was riveted by the faint wobble of his lower lip. It seemed odd that he should be alarmed merely because Ruan had intended to land there. 'What do you mean by saying it's your declared goal?' she asked, intrigued.

Ruan's sharp eyes swivelled to hers. 'I needed to bump up my flying hours. I elected to make what they call a "declared goal challenge". That means you say where you're going to land instead of letting the wind decide.' He smiled to himself, a secretive, smug smile that made her want to hit him. 'It takes some working out—wind velocity, which air band you select and so on. My plans had to be so good that I met no unforeseen dangers. I'm sure you get my drift, David,' he murmured, his eyes glittering.

Natasha tensed at the thickening atmosphere. Plans? Dangers? He wasn't talking about the flight, she thought, her mind racing with possibilities. This was to do with his real reason for being here. He did nothing without giving it careful thought first, however reckless his actions seemed. Yet it was quite a coincidence that he'd come at this time, just as she and David were getting together again. Fascinated, she hastily lowered her eyes when she saw that Ruan was frowning suspiciously at her.

'But to land at Tredinnick...' David cleared his throat and laughed a little hollowly. 'Rather stupid, wasn't it? Hardly a risk worth taking. Miscalculate and you're in the English Channel!'

'Or right up the creek,' said Ruan coolly. 'Dead from exposure, I reckoned, in seven minutes. Nice of you to care, considering the bad feeling between us.'

Natasha shuddered visibly, appalled at the thought that he might have killed himself for a stupid act of bravado. 'Oh, Ruan!' she cried tremulously. 'Whatever made you chance your life like that?'

'Sin,' he said cynically.

'Yours or someone else's?' she snapped, excessively irritated by his flagrant disregard for his own neck. 'You're not involved in smuggling again, are you? We told you the last time, we hate that filthy business! Go and spoil some other part of the world with your evil trade!' she seethed. 'Roseland's too special to be defiled!'

'Well,' he sighed regretfully, 'it *looks* as if you'll have your wish. Pleasant though it is to renew old acquaintances, I have to get the balloon back to Bristol. You'll be glad to see me go, I'm sure.'

David let out a low hiss of relief. 'Very,' he said curtly. 'Choose somewhere else next time you want to show off. Natasha and I——'

'Ah, yes,' grated Ruan, suddenly dropping his laid-back manner. 'Natasha and you! What is this cosy double act? I give you a choice of three answers: a lover's reunion, a straightforward business partnership, or sexual favours for cash. Which is it?'

Natasha set her mouth and reined in her indignation, waiting for David to defend her reputation. But he was silent, scowling at Ruan as if he didn't know what to answer. Driven to the limit by Ruan's accusation, she rested an affectionate hand on David's chest and said boldly, 'Work it out for yourself, Ruan.' And deliberately she wound her arms around David's neck, whispering in his ear, 'Pretend we're lovers. With any luck, he'll give up and go.'

'Darling,' murmured David, entering into the spirit of the pretence immediately. He took the opportunity to nibble her lobe.

'I don't think she likes that,' observed Ruan drily.

'Leave us alone,' demanded Natasha, wondering if he'd seen that she'd tensed very, very slightly. She didn't like it. She hated the pretence, the denial of the truth, her frightening physical need for Ruan.

David aimed a kiss at her cheek which she managed to avoid by leaning back and smiling idiotically, the misery that she couldn't feel anything for her dear friend welling up inside her in sickening waves. He'd shared some of her childhood too. Why, then, didn't everything in sight remind her of *him*?

Seeing Ruan's knowing, mocking smile of disbelief, she pressed firmly against David, feeling a blush creep up her face at the unfamiliar intimacy. It felt all wrong. Instead of the hard muscled body she'd felt when Ruan had hauled her against him, there was the soft give of cushioned flesh. David had put on weight, she thought, unhappily accepting another kiss.

'What a cold, calculating little bitch you are,' remarked Ruan cynically. 'You don't love him.'

'I do!' she declared vehemently. She loved him as a friend, as her protector...

'No. Your body's going into revolt,' Ruan said caustically. 'A child of three could tell that.' Awkward in her movements, trying harder, she clung to David, hating every second and wishing she was in Ruan's strong, secure and infinitely more natural embrace—but that he had David's solid, unwavering heart.

'Go,' she said huskily. 'We don't want you here. We want to make a life together and you're not included.'

He winced, and she remembered with some anguish how she'd felt when he'd been made an outcast from local society, shunned and loathed by everyone because of his suspected criminal activities.

'I doubt I ever was included,' he said laconically, his dark, blank eyes scanning the couple in front of him and coming to rest sardonically on David's apprehensive face. 'You and your cronies always mocked my parents' broken English and the fact that Father was a waiter. You mocked the way I dressed,' he said, his head held proudly, 'my very passion for life.' Natasha frowned, knowing nothing of this, but surprisingly David made no attempt to deny what Ruan was saying. 'I didn't give a damn what anyone thought about me then, and I don't now. But before I leave I have some questions I want to ask you, David,' he said softly.

'Put them in writing when you get back to Bristol,' snapped David. 'I want nothing to do with you.' He checked his watch and gave a start of simulated surprise. 'Is that the time? I have to go. I must dash over to the nursing home in Falmouth to see the night staff.'

'How admirably caring of you! Checking up on the elderly ladies' health, I suppose. And...perhaps their wealth?' suggested Ruan nastily.

David quivered and went white. 'Get out of my life! Cause trouble and I'll sue *you* for slander,' he hissed.

'I'd need to be closer than Bristol to cause trouble,' drawled Ruan.

'Yes. Thank God for inaccessible Cornish lanes,' David muttered. 'I'll call for you in the morning, Natasha—you can bring some of your things to the clinic.' He hastily gave her a brief kiss, his lips cold and trembling. 'About ten. 'Bye!'

'But I——' To Natasha's astonishment, he was already striding away and she wondered what had caused his abrupt departure.

'You know, he could win an Olympic medal with the speed of that walk,' observed Ruan sardonically. His speculative glance slanted in her direction. 'Considering the fact that he knows I'm an out-and-out bastard, isn't it odd that he should leave us together, just when I want to ask him some questions?'

She looked at him warily, thinking the same thing. 'He also knows I dislike you intensely and that you won't be here long,' she answered haughtily. 'Also, he has a high sense of duty,' she added. 'The home is very important to him.'

'Sure it is. It's a good source of income,' murmured Ruan insultingly. 'With which he's virtually bought you. You couldn't resist his money, could you?'

'Don't be ridiculous,' scorned Natasha. 'David's successful enough, and I imagine the home is worth a lot, but if I were a gold-digger I'd go for a millionaire, not a country lawyer.'

'He can lay his hands on a million and more,' said Ruan tightly. 'I know that, you know that. Maybe the only difference is that I know where it came from.'

'*David*?' she cried incredulously. 'Oh, Ruan, your imagination's running riot!'

'Not at all,' he said equably, though there was a hard line to his mouth and he sounded very sure of himself. 'He was wearing a hand-cut Italian suit which would have cost half a solicitor's annual income. His shoes were Ferragamo, his shirt Ralph Lauren.' Ruan's eyes seemed to increase in intensity. 'Now this is David we're talking about. A man not given to wild extravagances like me. He's slow, methodical and cautious to a fault. That means he's had a windfall so generous that expensive clothes won't even make a dent in them.'

'Decent clothes are a sound investment,' she demurred.

'To impress his country clients? A little over the top, I'd say,' drawled Ruan.

Natasha felt exasperated. 'Hasn't it occurred to you,' she said in a pitying tone, 'that he might have been left some money?'

'Go on,' encouraged Ruan.

'I'm sure the ladies in the nursing home must occasionally show their gratitude in their wills.'

His thin smile was chilling. 'It had occurred to me,' he said laconically. 'But there'd have to be a lot of money and a lot of grateful ladies, otherwise how could he afford to buy a brand new rag-top Merc as well?'

She started. It had looked expensive, though she hadn't recognised the make—it was dark and David had driven off so fast. 'Perhaps it was a present from a rich client.'

Ruan's face was inscrutable. 'I'm sure it was,' he retorted, softly vitriolic.

'What are you implying?' she asked hotly. 'Are you suggesting that he's brought undue pressure to bear on the residents of the home? Is that why you're here? To...?' Her voice died away and she looked at him in horror, seeing the hatred, the bitterness in his face. 'Oh, God!' she whispered. 'You *have* come to cause trouble for him!'

'Wouldn't I have arrived by car and gone to the nursing home in Falmouth to denounce him there?' he murmured. He assumed an arrogantly nonchalant pose, folding his arms across his massive chest and angling his head to one side as if challenging her to come up with an answer. His jacket zip had eased down to reveal the V of deeply tanned skin the colour of golden oak. She blushed to think that he wore nothing beneath the leather. That was why it had been so warm, so body-hugging.

Her instincts told her that he was offering her a riddle, fully expecting her to be incapable of solving it. That was how Ruan's mind worked. He gave his enemies chances, deliberately making his own role more difficult. She'd seen that ploy over and over again, when he'd run rings around the masters at school who'd had a 'down' on the non-conforming Ruan. He'd always got his revenge, no matter how long he'd had to wait to do so, she thought nervously.

'Maybe you didn't want anyone to know you'd arrived on Roseland,' she said slowly. 'Word would spread around like wildfire the minute you were sighted and everyone would lock up their daughters,' she added tartly. 'Well, if you mean to spread rumours, you'd better get on with it—you don't have much time left. But don't be surprised if no one believes you. We all know which of you is to be trusted.'

'You think you know,' he said drily.

'Oh, no, Ruan! You won't shake my belief in my friend. I won't believe anything bad about David,' she said firmly.

'I was afraid of that,' he drawled. 'But then, I would never have believed anything bad of you once. It took me a while before I'd accept that you had a mercenary streak.'

'That's unfair!' she cried.

'Is it? You said yourself you'd turned your back on Roseland to make yourself a fortune. Haven't you now traded yourself, body and soul, for a life of luxury with your dear old friend, your old flame? Isn't that the way you think? That people can be bought and sold?' he taunted. 'After all, you believed that you could buy *me* once.'

She felt the awful lurch of sickness in her stomach. 'That's only the interpretation you put on it,' she said unhappily. 'I wanted to help you. You'd told me that your father was dying of cancer, that you dearly wanted to make him proud of you before he died. I had savings. I knew your dream of having your own sub-aqua business. You needed the money——'

'Not at the expense of my pride!' he said, his upper lip curling. 'You insulted me with your offer.'

'But you were penniless——!'

'Dammit, Natasha!' he snapped. 'Did you want to humiliate me? I am a proud man. However poor I was, I'd never make my way on a woman's back!'

She winced. He'd been twenty, she seventeen, and she would have given him everything she had to make him happy. 'That was the beginning of our quarrels,' she said in a low voice.

'You'd questioned my manhood,' he growled.

'I did apologise. I was young, stupid and impulsive.' She raised her eyes to his. 'I only wanted to help.'

He gave a harsh, ironic laugh. 'Well, your insult had startling results. It drove me to work till I dropped,' he admitted.

'And you made a choice,' she said miserably. 'You leapt straight into the arms of a whole raft of shady characters. You made money fast, you made your father proud for a while, but at a terrible cost!'

'Yes!' he grated. His eyes blackened as if a storm-cloud had swept over them. His hands imprisoned her face in a grip of iron. 'Everything would have been fine, but for you. Without you opening your pretty little mouth and telling everyone that I'd been signalling that yacht from the shore and suggesting I was mixed up with smugglers, without your jealousy and suspicion, without you blindly trusting David, I would still be here, running my business, perfectly content.'

'No!' she whispered, terrified by his venomous hatred. His free hand clamped on her back and thrust her against his body. She felt the hard line of his arousal leaping against her pelvis and a quiver of sensual pleasure shook her body and made her groan in shame. A heaviness lay over his eyes and she felt her own lids half closing.

'I can't believe that despite all that,' he hissed, 'despite everything you've done to me, there's still one hell of a chemistry between us.'

'There isn't!' Her denial sounded weak even to her own ears. 'You know I despise you. Any man who behaves with such callous disregard for decency deserves contempt.'

'Then you should despise David,' he snarled.

Her eyes blazed with anger. 'You're jealous of him!' she yelled. 'You've always been jealous of the fact that he had money and you didn't, that people respected him——' She hesitated for a brief second and then plunged on, so desperate to escape from the terrible hold he had on her that she'd twist the truth fractionally. 'And you can't stomach the fact that David and I got together when you put your own evil ambition before our relationship,' she cried. 'You hate the idea that we were kissing behind your back——'

'I would like to break your neck,' he whispered. 'But I have a better revenge in store for you.'

'I don't deserve this treatment from you!' she said jerkily. 'I want——'

'What you want is irrelevant,' he growled. 'It's what *I* want that matters.' His tongue moistened his mouth in contemplation of her and she began to breathe heavily with fear, the pressure of his aroused body drawing her mind to her physical danger. 'Touching you, feeling you, smelling that fragrance on your skin has intoxicated my senses,' he muttered.

'No,' she mumbled, trying to pull away from the crushing grip on her jaw. Ruan had always been highly sexed, very passionate, but his affection for her had always held him back. Now, he was older, harder, crueller. Now he didn't care what he did to her any more. He had the eyes of a man who had no mercy. 'Please leave me alone!' she whispered.

'Why should I?' he murmured. 'When I have an overpowering urge to dominate you, to reduce you to my own basic, physical level where the mind and the emotions are meaningless? You too should experience this once in your life,' he said menacingly. 'The helpless surrender to desire. To be kissed till you can't breathe for passion, to be caressed till your skin aches, to hear the erotic pleasures I have waiting for you. And when I've finished every bone in your body and every inch of your flesh will be consumed with carnal lust. I want you,' he said hoarsely. 'And I'll have you. Before I leave.'

She would have fallen if he wasn't holding her so ruthlessly. Her body felt boneless from the glorious melting quality of Ruan's persuasive voice which flowed through her like molten gold. Her lips slowly parted, treacherously provocative, and blossomed into a high-arched, hungry bow. And she fought for the control of her mind, staring at Ruan's implacable face, her worst fears confirmed. He thirsted for a revenge of the kind that was making her skin crawl. He was a ferocious, unforgiving enemy.

His finger ran down the side of her face and touched the corner of her mouth. Free of his restraining grip, she jerked her head away, her hair flying in all directions—and he caught a hank of it, twining his fingers in the yellow silky strands and winding it up till his knuckles lay against her cheek and she was forced to look him in the eyes.

She licked her dry lips to speak. Ruan stood very still, totally self-assured, utterly intimidating. 'You can't stand there and calmly give me advance notice of your intentions!' she rasped out hoarsely. 'You're just trying to browbeat me.'

'Natasha,' he said with quiet confidence, 'I've mastered everything I've gone out to conquer. Mountains, jungles, seas, women.' His voice was soft, but his eyes... Natasha shuddered. Their message was clear. He hated her with a feeling so intense that he could hardly prevent himself from throttling her, then and there.

'You want me to eat dirt, to grovel, all because you think I caused your business to collapse with a mountain of debts and you were left with the daunting prospect of starting over again,' she accused.

'And because when my father died I saw not love in his eyes, but sorrow and shame that I'd brought disrepute on the family name!' snarled Ruan in fury.

'Ohhh! It wasn't my fault you'd been found out!' she cried, tears starting in her eyes because of the terrible anguish she saw etched in every line of his face. 'You got yourself into trouble! You were the one signalling your partners in crime! I'm *sorry* your father knew. I

wish he'd died ignorant of your vile activities. But don't
blame *me*!'

'I hold you totally to blame,' he grated. 'That's why
I'd love you to grovel. I want to see you trying to hang
on to the last tattered shreds of your self-respect, while
you're begging me——'

'I'll never, ever beg you for anything!' she cried, a
rush of anger flowing through every vein in her body,
releasing her from a state of numb shock. She wrenched
her hair from his grasp and tossed it back in defiance.

He smiled cruelly. 'Oh, you will, Natasha. You will.'

'I will not. I wouldn't dream of asking you for anything. I despise you too much,' she said with passion.
'I detest a vindictive nature.'

'Not as much as I do,' he answered, his voice unnaturally quiet.

She bridled with the injustice. 'If you're suggesting
that I've been vindictive——!'

'Suggesting?' repeated Ruan scornfully. The ice in his
voice froze her blood. 'My business was going well till
you decided that my long working hours were spent with
other women and you accused me of two-timing you,'
he ground out through his teeth. 'The next day I got a
visit from the police. Then came the revenue men. Then
the health and safety inspector——'

'Ruan!' she insisted vehemently. 'You had that stolen
stuff on your premises. You'd forgotten to check those
air cylinders. But I didn't split on you. It was nothing
to do with me!'

'Then,' he continued, steamrollering her protest, 'there
was that article in the local paper. "Local man's
rendezvous with drug smugglers off Cellars Beach",' he
quoted. 'Ruinous headline, Natasha. The bank fore-
closed on me immediately. If that wasn't the action of
a vindictive woman——'

'It might have been—but it wasn't me!' she cried in exasperation. 'I don't know how you could have thought that!'

Ruan's nostrils scrolled in scorn. 'Because when you doubted my fidelity and my honour, when you actually believed I'd be mixed up with an evil trade like drugs, I realised that you weren't as special as I'd thought,' he drawled, his eyes hooded and unreadable. 'You were just a shallow, self-seeking female who knew nothing of my inner character or principles.'

'The evidence——' she began breathily.

'—was overwhelming,' he finished softly. 'Yes, I know. Someone made damn sure of that. But I deserved total allegiance from the woman who professed to love me. You left the sinking ship at the first alarm and abandoned me to my fate. You were so hysterical, I wouldn't have put anything past you——'

She flushed. 'I was upset, not hysterical,' she said coldly. 'And since I saw a succession of long-legged blondes, brunettes and redheads having sub-aqua lessons from you, being helped, giggling, into wet suits—and then out of them again—and standing you drinks in the Rising Sun all evening while I languished on my own, I think I was entitled to wonder if I was being played for a mug!'

'I can't help it if I attract women,' he said dismissively. 'Any more than I can help the fact that they're never to be trusted and can't see what's beyond their noses.'

Natasha gave an exasperated snort. 'I saw very clearly!' she muttered. 'I might have been blind at first, but I soon realised why you were "working" all hours——'

'After David so kindly told you about my business dinner in Truro?'

'Business?' she scorned, hurting inside because all the terrible pain of the past was being dragged up again. 'He said the woman was all over you,' she grated.

Ruan shrugged. 'He lied. But how can I fight the word of the trusty David?' he said sarcastically. 'I'm not wasting my breath trying to convince you. But I will take whatever action I see fit.'

'So you are set on some kind of revenge. That's terribly childish,' she said contemptuously, selecting her words to annoy him.

'Revenge is a matter of honour to a Sicilian,' he said with soft menace. 'As for being childish...if you doubt the fact, I'll provide evidence that I'm every inch a man.' He was amused by her shocked reaction to his suggestion, the full sensual curve of his mouth drawing her eyes and sending scurries of alarm signals through her body.

She quivered, unwillingly fascinated by the almost overpowering sex appeal he projected through every pore of his body. 'I want nothing to do with you,' she whispered. Her face ached with the strain of maintaining a dignified hauteur, when her instincts told her to run. 'Even if you had ten years of your valuable time to spare nothing will persuade me that you're anything but an unmitigated crook who's not fit to gut fish!'

A small, assured smile lifted Ruan's lips. 'Can you lay your hand on your heart and say that when we kissed you felt no quivers of desire, no deep throbbing pulses vibrating through your body?' he murmured. 'Can you swear your heartbeats were absolutely even, your breathing regular? May I ask if your voice *normally* sounds as though it's projected through thick satin?'

She was silent, unable to deny the truth, blushing under his close, smirking scrutiny. Her body had betrayed her. Everything she'd felt, Ruan had been aware of. It was like being stripped naked in public to have her private feelings so ruthlessly listed.

He grinned wolfishly, his teeth dazzling white and even in the deepening gloom, and in her wretchedness she could tell that he was deliberately turning on every ounce of his magnetic sex appeal in an all-out attempt to bind her to him.

Her blue-grey eyes darkened to a liquid lead. She felt as if she were falling from a cliff into deep black water. His cheekbones stood out raw in the shadowy light, and the set of his jaw and the expression on his face told her he had made certain plans for her which he intended to carry out whether she liked it or not.

Slowly he removed his gauntlets and with numbing insolence let his fingers drift to where her skirt gave way to the gossamer-fine nylon stocking. She gulped, frozen with alarm. The muscles of her thigh tightened at his touch as if he'd branded her there——

And she ground her teeth at her stupid reaction because he'd noticed it and was mocking her with his wicked green eyes, his fingers continuing to examine her snagged stockings with deep, agonising interest. So she lifted her strangely leaden hand to slap his face and he caught it, moving back with a low laugh.

'Leave me alone! We were finished long ago!' she cried fervently. 'I obliterated you from my mind, Ruan. I was stupid enough to think you were my knight in shining armour till I discovered there wasn't anyone inside.' He gave an imperceptible flinch and she congratulated herself on wounding his pride. 'You think you're God's gift; well, I have news for you. Some people know how to treat women, how to be loving, tender and kind. But not you.'

'And David is a saint? You think that his affection for you is genuine?' he asked harshly. 'Doesn't it occur to you that he's always wanted everything I've ever had? He flaunted his money around at school, trying to buy my friends. He used possessions to get what he wanted—as he is now.'

'You diminish yourself in my eyes,' she said, miserable to discover how shallow Ruan really was. 'You've been resentful and bitter all along. Your motives have been based purely on envy. Oh, Ruan! I idolised you!'

'You fool!' he breathed with a soft savagery. The cold, intense stillness of his face terrified Natasha. The menace that hung in the air increased, second by second, as he gazed steadily at her and the silence built up till she felt like screaming. Then he inhaled deeply, scorn curling his upper lip. 'Be like me,' he muttered. 'Learn that even angels can be devils in disguise. I don't blame you for taking what you can get out of life, only for pretending to yourself that your morals are unimpeachable.' His hands held her shoulders firmly, the thumbs gently massaging the hollow beneath her collarbone in a maddening rhythm. 'How the world corrupts the innocent,' he mused.

'Please go,' she said, endeavouring to sound icy cold. Yet all the time she wanted to cry. He'd filled such a yawning gap in her life and then opened it up again. She'd never felt so lonely as she did now, the scorned object of his unjust contempt.

'I can't,' he said. 'Not without first making a phone call. Would you trust me to come in for a brief moment?'

'No,' she answered. 'That would be like the Sabine women inviting those sex-starved Roman rapists into their homes.'

To her surprise, his dark eyes glinted with humour. 'The women were abducted nevertheless,' he said lazily. 'By the most outrageous trickery. However, I do have to make that call in the next five minutes.'

'Tough,' she said haughtily, standing her ground.

'Then my retrieve-crew will assume the worst and call out the lifeboat. It'll be launched on a wild-goose chase— which you could prevent. Where's your civic duty?' he asked mildly. 'What about the unnecessary expense, and the fury of the men concerned? You know I have to make that call, Tash.'

She frowned. 'I can't believe you don't have a travelling phone in that flight bag, along with the champagne,' she challenged, hiding her triumph when his eyes narrowed in annoyance.

'I do,' he admitted. He met her gaze head-on. 'It's not working.'

She was not at all taken in by his lie. If she could only have a look in his bag, she could prove he was lying. Now *that* was an idea . . . 'I'd be mad to trust you in my house,' she said, weakening.

'But selfish to make the lifeboat turn out unnecessarily.'

'Oh, very well, I suppose you have to come in,' she grumbled. 'Don't get any ideas. Make sure your crew gets here as fast as possible. I don't like the thought of being under the same roof as you.'

He smiled faintly with a cool arrogance that was unnerving and she wondered whether she was being stupid to imagine that she could cope with Ruan when he'd sworn to seduce her. He might have only an hour to spare, but he'd use every second to the best advantage. She thought of all the stories she'd heard about women he'd used for his own ends, despoiled and abandoned, and her hand shook as she plunged the big iron key into the plank door.

CHAPTER THREE

THE little fisherman's cottage seemed more cramped than she remembered—even compared with her minute London flat. She knew why, though. Ruan loomed over everything, big and overpoweringly male. He dumped her cases at the bottom of the stairs and wandered around in the half-light, touching things as she had touched the stones and trees of Penmellin when she'd arrived, full of joy.

Cross that he'd spoiled her pleasure, she placed her bag of groceries on the scrubbed pine table. 'Smells a bit musty,' she frowned, wrinkling her nose.

'Didn't you give the letting agent any advance notice to air it?' asked Ruan casually, fingering the small boat he'd carved for her when they were at school.

She took it from him and, clenching her teeth, dropped it into the bin, turning away from its heart-rending reminder of lost innocence with despair. 'There wasn't much point,' she said curtly. 'I'm going to David's tomorrow.'

'So you really are throwing in your lot with him,' he said softly.

Natasha withstood his level gaze, acting on the impulse of an idea that had come to her. Now she could separate him from his flight bag and she'd know if he was lying to her or not.

'I am, so get used to that. You might do the decent thing and take my luggage upstairs while I light the candles,' she said, hoping that had sounded ungracious enough not to be suspicious. 'And find the luggage stand for me.'

That would take him ages, she thought with satisfaction. She kept it under the bed. When he was safely upstairs, she eagerly unstrapped his bag and peered inside. Taking out the two champagne bottles, two carefully boxed glasses, a pot of fine Russian caviare, fresh rolls and half a bottle of whisky, she identified what was left: a two-way radio, a compass and an altimeter, a first-aid box and finally a map of the area showing Tredinnick House. And Penmellin Cove, ringed in red ink.

'So,' she said thoughtfully to herself. 'You did intend to land at Penmellin. Why?' And why, she wondered, as she traced the flight path, did it appear as if he'd taken off a mere mile away?

Mystified, she pushed buttons on the radio and it crackled. It was working. Her expression became grim. Remembering their exact positions, she replaced the items she'd removed and did up the bag again then sat back on her heels, trying to make sense of the facts.

He'd been deceiving her. He'd meant to land at Penmellin even though that was more difficult a feat to achieve than a touch-down in a Tredinnick field. Penmellin was more remote, tucked down at the bottom of the valley and isolated, whereas Tredinnick land was closer to other houses. Odd.

Her heart began to thump. He hadn't known she'd be there. It seemed as if he had returned—perhaps to use her cottage as a remote, unvisited base, to do some illicit smuggling. And she was now in the way. Her forehead puckered. Yet he was intending to go back to Bristol tonight. It didn't make sense.

Lighting the candles and unpacking the food she'd bought in Truro that afternoon for her supper and breakfast, she suddenly realised that Ruan had been gone rather a long time.

'Hurry up! You've got a phone call to make!' she yelled. Her alerted ears heard the soft closing of the latch on her bedroom door, then water sluiced down the pipes from the bathroom.

'Coming!' Ruan hurried down the stairs, his face as innocent as a child's. 'No towels,' he said, waving wet hands.

Highly suspicious, she brought a faintly damp one from the airing-cupboard. He'd been in her bedroom all that time. Doing what? He thought she was stupid, she thought crossly, her pride ruffled. He'd learn different, she vowed to herself.

'I'm making tea. Want some?' she asked casually, intending to use the time to question him.

'Tea? God, Tash, where's your sense of adventure?' he scathed. 'Live dangerously. Crack open this bottle while I contact my crew.' He undid his bag and handed the champagne to her with the two glasses, a look of devilish challenge on his handsome face.

'I don't mind,' she said with a shrug of indifference. It suited her purpose. In no time at all she had to sweeten him up—and alcohol would help to relax him. A mischievous and determined light glowed in her eyes.

Ruan's grin flashed briefly then he turned his back and dialled a number while Natasha listened unabashed.

'Caroline?' he murmured seductively into the receiver. 'Sure I'm safe... No, a bit bruised. The landing was spectacular—surprisingly soft. I'm in a place called Penmellin, just below Tredinnick. There's only one cottage. Got it...?' He chuckled sexily, as if the woman had said something flirtatious. 'Of course,' he drawled lazily. 'Where are you?'

Natasha scowled at the bottle and eased out the cork, wondering as she poured the bubbling liquid into the two champagne flutes who the devil Caroline was. Silently she passed Ruan a glass and slumped in a comfortable armchair, suddenly feeling rather tired and a little nervous of pumping him for information.

'What?' barked Ruan down the phone. Natasha barely bothered to look up. 'Well, get yourself on the right road... Half an hour?' He groaned and slammed the receiver into the cradle irritably.

'It's all right,' she told him, making her voice grudging. 'You can stay till your...friend arrives to pick you up.'

'Thanks.' He made no move towards her, but went to the window and stared out unseeingly into the darkness.

Natasha felt sufficiently reassured to relax her guard. With Caroline on her way, he wouldn't try anything stupid. She could hold out for half an hour. The exhaustion seeped through her whole body as if the blood could barely manage to creep through her veins. She stretched out her long legs, feeling every muscle was aching. Her eyes closed and she took a long swallow of the champagne and a deep, relaxing breath.

It was, she supposed hazily, the cumulative effect of the long hours without a proper break that she'd worked ever since she'd been in London. For all that period, she'd pushed herself to the limits, working all hours to fill the emptiness of life without Ruan, forcing herself into an existence which held no magic, no love and no excitement, paying the price in violent headaches and periods of crucifying self-pity.

'I'll light the wood-burner.'

She nodded slowly at Ruan's quiet suggestion. 'Please.'

He crumpled newspaper and fed it into the huge cavity of the iron stove, laying on the kindling in a deft, accurate formation guaranteed to get the maximum heat from the slightly damp wood. Bonfires were his speciality, she thought bitterly, watching him heave a massive log on to the leaping flames. He'd set enough fires going in local women to have warned the Spanish Armada. Better to stay damp and cold than to burn and be destroyed, she mused.

The kindling was almost spent now and her last sight
of the great pine log before Ruan slammed the heavy
iron doors shut was that it was stolidly resisting the
flames. If only she had! When Ruan had hurt her, she'd
understood for the first time why her mother had never
shown emotion or tenderness. It simplified life.

Her mother had been hurt by losing the man she'd
loved too, when her father had drowned in the Carrick
Roads, his stern trawler capsizing while it ran for shelter
to St Mawes harbour. It had left her, an impressionable
six-year-old, with a new fear of the sea and a mother
who'd decided overnight that nothing would touch her
again.

'Anything else I can do?' he asked softly.

'No,' she answered huskily.

'I'd forgotten how quiet it was here,' he murmured,
looking at her strangely.

She gave a wistful smile. 'Too quiet for you, I expect.'
The depth of the silent night was intensified by the
glowing warmth in the cosy room. Outside was total
blackness. In London the glow from street lights would
have spread for miles around.

That bustling world seemed far away. Since her quarrel
with Ruan, oddly enough, her career had gone from
strength to strength. First there'd been the job in the
small Chelsea salon and then as a highly paid hairdresser for a major chain of beauty specialists. And now
David had given her this wonderful chance.

'Your glass is empty.'

'Thanks.' Preoccupied with her thoughts, she held it
out while Ruan refilled it. David had been generous in
thinking of her. He'd kept in touch ever since she'd left,
informing her of the scandals that had come to light
involving Ruan and obviously anxious that she should
know she'd done the right thing by exposing his criminal
activities to the public.

'Natasha.'

Ruan; silent, stealthy, making her jump, opening another bottle and coming to sit on the arm of her chair, topping up her drink. Another bottle? she thought blearily. What had happened to the first? To avoid his curious eyes, she sipped with pretended enjoyment and realised that her head was swimming from the lack of food and sheer exhaustion.

'I'm getting light-headed. I've got to eat something,' she mumbled, knowing she must make some kind of conversation with him if she was to discover his real intentions.

He put his hand on her slender shoulder, preventing her from rising. 'In a moment,' he soothed. 'You look tired. Rest for a while first, then I'll get you something if you like.'

His hand began to stroke her forehead. It was wonderful. She might disarm him if she appeared to be bowled over by his charms. With a sigh, she leant her head back while his gentle fingers massaged her temples. She knew the skills of massage herself: she'd taken several courses in beauty therapy. Ruan was as good as the girls in the salon and she wondered jealously if he'd learnt his technique from a masseuse in some strip joint.

'Ruan,' she said, frowning and trying to sit up. 'I don't think—ohhh...' she whispered helplessly, her voice trailing away.

'Does that help? You looked so tense,' he husked, his mouth perilously close to her ear. His fingers had dropped to her neck, working the muscles of the shoulders. And... She tried to focus her mind. He was slowing all her senses down, making her mind drift peacefully with his seductive caresses. 'I'm glad we've met again,' he whispered. She thought she felt a kiss on the top of her head, but wasn't sure.

'Coincidence,' she mumbled thickly.

'Mmm. Amazing.'

His mouth swam into view, dark, intense, his eyes compelling, his mouth... She swallowed, feeling an uncontrollable urge to kiss the softly smiling lips. Oh, Ruan, she groaned inside. Don't do this to me...

'Please stop,' she protested weakly.

'I have a problem,' he murmured, lifting the hair from the nape of her neck and cradling the back of her skull in his hands.

So have I, she thought hazily. A problem keeping my mind razor-sharp. 'Tell me,' she managed, hoping he'd confide in her.

She blinked. His mouth was a fraction away from hers. Maybe she shouldn't have encouraged him to come in. He'd never impart any information, not without exacting a heavy price.

'It's my bruises. They're very painful,' he said huskily.

'Oh!' she cried in consternation, sitting more upright and rocking with the waves of dizziness that resulted. She gritted her teeth. 'You should have said!' she mumbled indistinctly. 'Where? Let me see to them.'

'Generous of you, in the circumstances,' he murmured.

She noticed blood on his hand and her brow furrowed at the overwhelming urge to touch his palm with her mouth. 'I don't see why,' she croaked, and endeavoured valiantly to pull herself together. 'We were friends once. I'd do the same to anyone who fell out of a balloon into my front garden,' she added caustically.

He smiled thinly. 'Even the man who wasn't fit to lick the feet of a leper?' he asked in a low tone.

Natasha flushed with embarrassment. 'I was young and angry when I said that——'

'And full of passion.'

She quivered at the deep richness of his velvet voice that caressed every inch of her body. 'Passion is a waste of time,' she muttered.

'No. Passion is the essence of life.'

He stood up and unzipped his jacket. The breath seemed unable to leave her lungs. He was bare-chested as she'd thought, the beautiful gold of his Mediterranean skin gleaming like rich satin. Her eyes fell to the darkening bruises around his rapidly rising and falling ribcage.

'Oh, you are hurt!'

'When I breathe,' he said softly, kneeling in front of her, 'the pain seems to get worse. You'd think it would ease, but it doesn't. Can you do something about it?'

'I—I...'

She stopped trying to speak. Her ribs hurt too. She wanted healing, but that was nothing to do with a self-inflicted injury like Ruan's. Once, he had torn out her insides and caused her terrible pain so physical that she hadn't been able to eat or sleep for days. She'd cried all the tears from her body, used up a lifetime's quota. There was nothing left but an empty hollow where love and tenderness had once thrived.

He reached out and dragged the flight bag towards him, never taking his brooding eyes from her for a second. Unerringly he found the first-aid kit, placing it on her lap.

'What do you want me to do?'

'Pardon?' she husked, her mouth dry. Hastily she moistened her throat with more champagne and regretted it immediately, her limbs seemingly filled with wool.

'Would it be easier if I lay down?' he asked.

Knowing the danger in that, she shook her head, reading the labels on the plastic containers with a slow, stupid deliberation because she was finding it hard to concentrate on what she was doing. She tipped witch-hazel on to cotton wool and hesitantly dabbed at the bruises, her hands shaking. Ruan groaned and her fingers faltered, spilling some liquid on to his thighs.

'Oh, I'm sorry!' she cried, wiping the stain on the smooth, tightly stretched leather with her handkerchief. Someone had lit a torch inside her loins. Her hands stilled, the warmth of his thighs burning into her fingertips and she flung him a look of pure confusion.

Ruan growled in his throat, caught her hands to pull her towards him and fell back to the floor with Natasha on top. His mouth was everywhere: her forehead, her cheeks, her throat, her lips...

'Natasha,' he whispered. 'I want you. God, how I want you!'

His hands were running up and down her body feverishly. 'No, Ruan, no,' she moaned. But he ended her complaints with a kiss so passionate and desperate that it left her gasping.

'Yes, oh, God, yes!' he insisted savagely, his fierce eyes glittering with excitement. He held her face between the warm palms of his hands and she believed that he could crush her bones if he chose. His lids lowered drowsily as he contemplated her mouth and Natasha felt a spear of wanting slice through her defenceless body.

Slowly, with infinite and elaborate care, he brought her mouth to his, softly pressing his lips to hers with the lightest of touches. Feather-light kisses followed the outline of her mouth and then there was the moist teasing of his tongue coaxing it open.

She pushed against his chest and drew back, her eyes as troubled as a storm-tossed sea. 'No!' she said sharply. 'I don't know what you're doing, Ruan, but——'

'I do. Let me show you.'

Helplessly, appalled by the fact that her body had conquered her mind, she felt his hand gently unpicking the buttons of her tightly fitting jacket. And she let him. Like a stupid, lovesick groupie, she seemed unable to stop him, even though she knew he must think she was easy prey and loathed herself for wanting his touch on her heated body more than she valued her own self-respect.

'Natasha!' he whispered hungrily, undoing the last button. 'So little time...'

Her body chilled and the turmoil in her head cleared with the cold truth. Time? Oh, yes; any moment now and sweet Caroline would sashay through the door! Talk about double-dating! If his neck weren't so sinewy, she'd wring it! She would stop at nothing—almost, she amended—to cut the conceited Ruan Gardini down to size.

Allowing her lashes to sweep down, she sighed wistfully. 'I want...' She let her throaty voice drift into the silence.

His mouth drew deeply on the flesh of her neck. 'What?' he muttered indistinctly.

'Tea. I'm parched.' Aided by his total surprise, she evaded his clutches by rolling off him quickly and shakily stumbled over to the kitchen cupboard.

'That's an old trick,' he drawled, quite unconcerned.

'It's the only one I know,' she said grimly, still surprised at how easily she'd broken free.

Ruan eased himself into a sitting position, closely watching every move she made till her fingers seemed to have grown eight thick thumbs. Clumsily she ladled tea-leaves into the pot, spilling some on the table. He came over and brushed them into his hand and she almost smashed the lid when she jammed it on the pot, because his hunky chest was too close and too touchable and too darn naked for her liking.

'You're nervous.'

'Tired,' she retorted, offering him a forced, innocent smile, 'and you've poured champagne into me so I'm not entirely steady. Ruan, what——?'

'Careful,' he murmured. 'Dangerous water.' He took the kettle from her wavering hand and filled the teapot to the brim. 'You could have burned yourself,' he said softly. 'While that brews, I'll roll up my balloon. And then I'll be back.'

'Don't bother. Your crew's coming,' she said, a little desperate.

'Yes. But I could stay if you want me to.'

She blinked at his casual offer of sex. 'Oh! No!'

'You do want me. That was plain enough. Surely you're not worried that David might find out we'd spent the night together?' he murmured.

'The night——?' She found herself woefully unable to form the words she wanted to speak. Confused, she wished she had Ruan's calculating mind. Then she'd be able to twist him around her little finger and find out what she wanted to know. In the meantime, she had to play for time. String him along for the next ten minutes or so. 'I'd be a fool to rock the boat.'

'So there's no love involved between you two.'

'None—other than that for an old friend,' she admitted.

'I'm grateful for your frankness,' he drawled. 'At least I know it's his money that attracts you, and not the man himself. Perhaps when you know he's even more of a bastard than I am——'

'No,' she frowned. 'I won't believe that of anyone.'

His mouth twisted wryly. 'I ought to force you to listen to me,' he growled. 'Remember Winifred?'

She looked puzzled. Ruan seemed to be watching her with unusual attention as if he'd expected some kind of action. 'Of course,' she said. 'At the home. I used to do her hair, free of charge. You took her out on trips.' Her face gentled. It had been an odd friendship—the bad-boy Ruan and the sweet old lady. She searched his face for clues but found none. The temptation to know what he was up to grew stronger every minute. 'I intend to visit her while I'm here. Do you know if she's still alive? You've been writing to her?'

'Off and on. However, I believe she's been moved somewhere—I've heard nothing for two months,' he said with a menacing softness. 'She's very sweet and helpless, isn't she? An eighty-year-old with the mental age of ten. No living relatives. Sad and vulnerable,' he mused idly. 'Easily taken advantage of by the unscrupulous.'

Her eyes widened. 'You're not suggesting that David's done something illegal?' she cried in astonishment.

'Who, Mr Clean himself?' mocked Ruan. 'We all know what a highly respected man he is,' he said with a sarcastic sneer. 'A specialist in Court of Protection work, representing people who are incapable of handling their own affairs—people who can't sign cheques, minors, wards of court, the mentally ill...'

'Like Winifred,' she observed, wondering what he was driving at.

'Exactly. I imagine that he's asked a judge to make a will on her behalf.'

'David's decent like that,' she said warmly. 'Though Winifred can't have many possessions.'

'Who knows? Do you think they'll be left to David?' he enquired silkily.

She took a deep, shaky breath, her face filled with horror. 'You're insinuating——!'

'We must meet again and talk about old times, Tasha. Would you like that?' he murmured. His hands pushed back her hair, his fingers lingering on the satiny skin below her ears, massaging gently with a maddeningly rhythmic movement.

Her mind whirled with the veiled hints he'd made. She owed it to David to discover how far Ruan would go in the pursuit of his revenge—if he'd try to spread this ridiculous story involving Winifred and David's integrity.

'I——' She quivered from the pressure of Ruan's fingers, her body suffering from his practised assault. And she gave in to her impulse to tip her head back in wanton pleasure and let a soft moan escape her lips. It would fool him. Or...was she fooling herself? she thought hazily. 'We could meet again,' she said shakily, reluctant to annoy him—yet.

Briefly his lips touched hers and it seemed to Natasha that he had to make a huge effort of will to draw away. 'I knew the old hot-blooded Natasha lay simmering under that layer of frost,' he murmured. His hand ran insolently down her body and she suffered its crude assault in grim silence. 'We'll have a good time together. And David will never know.'

'Oh, no, I—I mean...it could be a while before I'm free,' she mumbled, wishing her mind was clearer. 'I'll be settling in, and so on. But I'm dying to hear what you've been up to, where you've travelled and so on. Tell me now,' she urged. 'Tell me what your plans are, like——' She cleared the lump from her throat as she delved into the blissful past. 'Like the time we sat in that cellar, and bared our souls,' she said with an attempt at a smile.

'"Curiosity killed the cat",' he said, and Natasha's eyes narrowed because there was a faint threat in the way he'd said that. He grinned expansively. 'But I'll tell you everything you want to hear after I've seen to the balloon.'

Her thoughts racing, she stretched her lips in a big, silly smile and watched him walk jauntily out of the cottage. Immediately he'd gone, her expression became worried. If he knew what she was up to, he'd show no mercy. He lived life in the fast stream, risking his neck over and over again. And that meant he held life cheaply and had nothing to lose. Her palms began to sweat.

A chill settled on her body, damping it like a sea-fog, and she feared that if she didn't stop him he'd keep returning to cause trouble for David and herself till he'd achieved his purpose. Because he never gave up.

Natasha watched Ruan hang the oil lamp on the side of the basket and begin to spread the balloon flat. Her eyes lingered on the breadth of his shoulders, the flexing of his thigh muscles as he moved and the deft, confident movements of his hands. And she had a gnawing ache in the pit of her stomach merely from looking at him.

There was something oddly appealing about the angle of his jaw and the line of his profile that made her want to run out and touch him; to run her fingers down the smooth forehead and along the ridge of each thick black brow, following the line of his vigorously waving hair.

'Tasha!' he yelled. He was crouching down, holding on to a concertina of material, beckoning her, and she opened the door to hear him clearly. 'I can't do this on my own! Come and help.'

'All right,' she called reluctantly. 'Wait while I change. I don't want this suit to be a total write-off.'

When he stood up, tall and dishevelled, and grinned his thanks, her heart pounded. But she told herself firmly as she ran up the stairs—dismayingly like a girl going out on her first date with the school hero—that she must remember she was playing with a venomous rattlesnake by taking him on at his own game, even for a mercifully short time.

'What are you doing in there? Hurry up!'

Struggling into her jeans, she flung open the window beneath the heavy slate overhang. '*Wait*, you impatient devil!' she grumbled. Then a wary look came into her eyes. 'What's the matter?' she asked, puzzled by the ominous way he stared at her.

'You are,' he said shortly. 'With your hair all tousled you look as if you've just jumped out of bed. Come down before I forget Caroline, and join you.'

She shut the window so hastily that the panes rattled in the lead lattice and was passing the bed on her way out when something odd caught her eye. Ruan hadn't found the luggage stand after all, but had placed her cases on the mattress. So what had he been doing while he was up here?

Frowning at one open case as if it would give her some clue, she suddenly gasped aloud. 'Well, I'll be darned! You prying, snooping . . . !'

Beautifully arranged, her silk trouser suit lay exposed in all its glory, now she'd whisked out the jeans and baggy jumper she'd thrown in at the last minute. But she never folded her clothes arms-to-middle like that.

Her trembling fingers worked through the contents and found what she'd been looking for—a chiffon scarf tucked almost unnoticeably into the middle layers. It had held her few items of dress jewellery—earrings and a couple of necklaces. Now they were scattered on the skirt beneath and resting on her well-thumbed address book that Ruan had given to her on her sixteenth birthday. Only someone riffling through the contents of her case would have inadvertently dislodged the jewellery.

'Well!' she murmured, baffled by the discovery. 'Curiouser and curiouser!'

'I did warn you.'

She gave a little scream and jumped back. Ruan's big body filled the small doorway, and his expression was no longer friendly. His eyes flickered for a split second to the opened case and she knew he was wondering if she'd noticed anything.

Plastering a smile on her face, she tried to look penitent. 'Sorry!' she said nervously. 'You surprised me——'

'It's how I operate,' he said laconically. 'By catching people unawares.'

She swallowed, and put the smile back. 'It's years since I was here. Everywhere I turn there are memories.' She cast around hastily for proof of her excuse. 'The shells,' she gabbled, picking them up and handing them to him. 'Porthbeor Beach. I thought of the dolphins we saw. I keep going back in time——'

'Big mistake,' he said quietly, dropping them unseen on the bed. 'It never was as good as we think it was. It's fatal to build illusions on the belief that the sun always shone and everyone had fun.' His face grew still, his eyes brooding. 'Much of the past was grim.'

Her eyes widened. 'Grim? You had a tough life, but you seemed always so... buoyant, bounding around without a care in the world, full of enthusiasm——'

'You saw what everyone else saw. And what I wanted everyone to see,' he said flatly.

'I had no idea. What was grim, Ruan?' she prompted gently, surprised that there had been a side to his life he'd never confided in her despite their years of friendship. No, she mused, Ruan was secretive even with his intimate friends. He held part of himself back and always would.

He seemed to be weighing up whether to confide in her or not and she held her breath. He tossed back one heavy lock that kept sweeping on to his forehead in a well-remembered gesture of impatience.

'Quite a few things,' he answered, his expression brooding and far-away, as if he hardly knew she was there. 'People see what they want to see, not the raw, harsh reality.'

'You have always had a loving mother, with a generous heart,' she reminded him, her face earnest. 'It was like clambering into a warm blanket, entering your home,' she said wistfully. 'Mine was cold and dead in comparison. Isn't that real enough for you?'

He paused, his shoulders lifting as if emotion was claiming him but when he spoke his voice was steady. 'It seemed like paradise to you, I know. I even thought it was, for a while. But hell wasn't very far beneath. It never is,' he said cynically. 'Mother sometimes cried at night when she thought I was asleep. She used to worry over the pile of bills littering the table.'

'Oh, Ruan, I'm so sorry. It must have been an awful struggle for her,' she ventured quietly, her heart wrung with the image he'd conjured up. 'But she can't have been that badly off. She had two jobs, cleaning and cooking at the home with my mother, and serving behind the bar at the Rising Sun.'

'It wasn't well-paid work. And Father had ploughed money into the bistro where he worked. It went bust. And then his treatment ate up our savings.'

'I see,' said Natasha gently. 'She should have come to my mother for help. Or perhaps David's—she had a lot of money.'

'My mother had her pride. Anyway, can you honestly see either of them showing generosity to us?' he asked sardonically. His hand touched her tumbled hair in a gesture that was almost affectionate. 'Only you ever showed compassion. You and your father.'

'Oh! You remember him?' she cried eagerly.

'A bit. He taught me to sail.' He hesitated, his gaze slewing in her direction speculatively. 'He was open and honest as the day is long. Everyone respected him.' His mouth twisted cynically. 'So much for genes,' he muttered.

Natasha winced, cut to the quick. 'Shall we get your balloon folded?' she asked in a hard tone to disguise her bitterness.

'Anything's better than having a heart-to-heart, isn't it?' he said sardonically.

As they worked together, rolling up the material, Natasha tried to interrogate Ruan. 'What's your job now?' she asked as casually as she could. Vaguely she recalled that Bristol was quite a magnet for balloonists. 'Are you training to be a balloon pilot?'

'Brushing up skills,' he said laconically, leaving her none the wiser. 'That's why I took the gamble of this flight—to test myself. But you know me, I've been a gambler since I could work out the odds. The wind blowing up the Percuil river gave me some problems and I thought I'd better come down before I ran out of land.'

'What would have happened if you had?' asked Natasha soberly, her mouth suddenly very dry. 'Was David right about the danger?' However short his flight had really been, it must have been risky.

He turned his calculating eyes on her. 'If I'd come down in the sea or the Fal estuary, I would have drowned,' he said in an offhand tone.

'Like Father,' she whispered, her eyes flickering with pain.

'Damn! Sorry I reminded you,' he frowned.

Her mouth quivered. 'Don't apologise to me, apologise to your mother for what you must be doing to her now!' she muttered crossly, helping him to stow the balloon in the big canvas bag. Why did he seek to destroy people by his actions? 'Can't *you* see further than your own nose? Do you have to behave recklessly and selfishly? Every time you flirt with death, your mother dies a little——'

'She *is* dead,' he said in an emotionless voice.

Soberly she studied his face. He'd idolised his mother. The grief didn't show and she marvelled at his control. And feared it. 'I am really sorry. How long ago?' she asked huskily.

He was busy fiddling with the burner unit. 'Some months after my business crashed and I went bankrupt,' he muttered.

'What happened?' she mumbled unhappily.

'I don't know. Heart attack. I was in Bolivia at the time.'

'Doing what?' she frowned. 'How could you leave her at such a time to go on a jaunt for your own pleasure?' she cried. 'It was thoughtless! I imagine you were hell-bent on testing your wretched boundless courage!'

'No. I was searching for wild flowers,' he growled. 'What do you think?'

'I think you're probably beyond salvation,' she snapped.

'That's why I can act without restraint,' he said softly, and she felt a cold shiver go down her back. 'Don't forget that I have absolutely nothing left to lose, since my reputation's shot to pieces—thanks to you.'

'I've already explained——' she began.

'And that makes it all right?'

'Oh, Ruan,' she said with a huge sigh. 'We could go round and round in circles on this one. I truly regret everything that's happened. It hasn't been easy for me either. I have missed Penmellin and everything here. Look, we don't have long before we part again,' she said despondently. 'Can't we spend the last few minutes together without hurling accusations at each other?'

Ruan hesitated and then shrugged his shoulders. But when they sat at the kitchen table he accepted a mug of tea from her without any sarcastic comments at all. His eyes were solemn over the rim as he drank. 'To old times,' he said quietly.

'To the future,' she amended, angling for an opening.

'I'll drink to that,' he agreed. 'So. You're making an alliance with David. Will you work? Or lie back and enjoy the fruits of life?'

This could be her last chance to discover some clue that would tell her what he meant to do. Her lowered eyes stayed fixed on the pattern she was tracing on the smooth pine table-top and he would never know from the bright way she replied that her heart was bumping with nerves.

'I'll go on working. Nothing interesting about that. What about you?' She tried to look casual, woman-of-the-world, and gave a rueful laugh. 'How's the gun-running?' she joked, knowing he'd never be involved in arms-dealing. 'Or is it whisky?' she teased.

'I'm involved in a wide range of activities. I must admit, I get chased too often for my liking,' he offered, a small smile playing about his lips.

'Oh, Ruan!' she said reproachfully. 'You're—you're not still mixed up in drugs, are you?'

'That's like the old question, "Have you stopped beating your wife?"' he said drily. 'I could deny my lurid past, but you wouldn't believe a word I said, would you?' He tapped her reprovingly on the nose and then let his finger wander to her mouth. She pulled back with a jerk. 'Is it just David's manly charms and his wealth that's brought you back?' he asked absently, his eyes riveted to her parted lips.

'Mainly a golden opportunity,' she said, desperately trying to get his mind off sex. 'As you've gathered, David has asked me to be his partner,' she said, with a passable stab at simpering bashfulness.

She sneaked a look at Ruan to see how he'd taken her deliberate fudging of the truth. Partnership with David was commercial, but she hoped her remark had been vague enough to mislead. She was rewarded with a tightening of his expressive mouth.

'You'd let him make love to you for the sake of some better quality clothes on your back?' he asked scathingly.

Natasha was fed up with beating around the bush. It wouldn't matter if she told Ruan what she meant to do. 'I'm considering the job of beauty therapist in a health clinic he's almost set up,' she explained.

'Money, perhaps the prospect of a brilliant marriage, and now gainful employment. How could you refuse?' he murmured. 'No wonder you left your job in London. Where exactly is this clinic?' he asked idly.

She frowned, then gave a little awkward laugh. 'Now I come to think of it, David's never actually made that clear,' she said, feeling rather a fool. 'In Falmouth somewhere, I suppose. He lives there—and the nursing home is there too, of course.' Thinking of the pleasant life she could build for herself back on her home ground, she let her guard drop without realising it, a slow, dreamy smile spreading over her face. 'It's everything I've ever wanted,' she said gently.

'As I thought. The lure of gold,' he said cynically.

'No,' she denied. 'Fondé.' Her brow puckered and she looked at him in dismay. 'I'm not supposed to have told you that,' she said anxiously. 'I'm not usually indiscreet——'

'Are you talking about the French cosmetics people?' he asked.

'*The* cosmetics giant,' she answered hesitantly. 'Oh, well, in for a penny, in for a pound. I do want you to understand why I've thrown everything up and come back to Roseland. It's not what you've been thinking. This is a fabulous opportunity for me. We're being considered as the first British outlet for their *Trésor enterré* range. Buried treasure,' she translated unnecessarily. 'Everything's made from natural products—plants and herbs from all around the world.'

'Impressive,' he said admiringly. 'Even I have heard of these people. So David's cashing in on the back-to-nature movement. It's a franchise you're buying, then? Expensive?'

'Oh, incredibly!'

'If *you* use the stuff, I can see that it works,' he commented, brushing strands of hair from her face and studying it intently.

She suffered his exploration in silence. But when he leaned closer and she felt the soft hiss of his breath fanning her face, and when the air was filled with the tantalising aroma of his aftershave, she glanced nervously at her watch.

'Your friend's late.'

'Mmm.' Ruan brushed the back of his hand down her soft cheek, around her chin. His fingers caressed her throat. 'Your face is without a flaw,' he observed softly.

'Y-y-yes. I have to look after it in my job.'

'Awful if it was damaged.'

His remark hung in the air menacingly. Natasha's frightened eyes lifted to his. There was nothing but a blank screen as if he'd wiped out all personal emotion and replaced it with black ice.

CHAPTER FOUR

FOR a moment, Natasha's fear prevented her from speaking. 'I see no reason why my face should be damaged,' she husked eventually.

'Depends what risks you take with it,' he drawled.

'How can I be risking it if I work for David?' she asked, but her intended bravado came out in a quavering croak.

'I would imagine that the volatile oils you use in the beauty business are quite inflammable,' he said with devastating casualness.

Her tea slopped and she put the cup down, staring blindly at her wet, shaking fingers. Her wrist was lifted in the air and she found that Ruan was methodically wiping each finger with his handkerchief.

'I suppose it would give you pleasure to set fire to the clinic,' she scorned, trying in vain to snatch her hand away. 'What extraordinary ambitions you have! Ruan the Destroyer! At least what I'm doing will benefit people!'

His fingers gripped hers cruelly. 'People destroy themselves without any help from me,' he said cynically. 'And forgive me, but would you like to explain how creams and face masks are beneficial to womankind?'

'Certainly. I will relieve you of some of your ignorance,' she said, goaded into standing up for what she believed in. 'Fondé have done a great deal of research into healing plants found in remote jungles—the same places where you whiz around shooting parrots and rapids for fun!'

'You mean . . . if I'd kept my eyes open, I might have met some of your beauty researchers, tramping through the undergrowth?' he asked in an infuriatingly sarcastic manner. 'What a small world it is, to be sure!'

She shot him an angry glare. 'I doubt they'd ever notice someone like you. They're serious, dedicated people—the best. Fondé take the cream of the world's researchers and I admire the company for doing so.' He seemed to be hiding a small smile and that only made her more irritated. 'That's why the products have an outstanding international reputation,' she snapped. 'Not only in the beauty field, but in corrective cosmetic treatment, too. David's basing his whole advertising campaign on them.'

'I'm delighted to hear that,' he nodded approvingly.

'And you ought to know,' she added proudly, 'that their products have the most wonderful results on burns patients and people with disfiguring birthmarks. It's David's dream and mine to win the franchise and we're both very excited about it. The clinic will be a haven for the scarred: mentally, physically or emotionally,' she explained with immense satisfaction.

'It all sounds utterly worthy.'

She was disappointed by his detached response. 'You don't have to mock because I have ideals,' she said resentfully.

'Ideals are fine, providing no one stops you attaining them.'

Her eyes widened at the implication. Taking a deep breath, she decided to face him out with her suspicions. 'You won't——' She quailed. Ruan's eyes looked very hard suddenly. 'Oh, God, Ruan! You won't try to damage David's venture in any way, will you?' she asked shakily. 'He's worked so hard, probably put all his money into it . . .' Her voice trailed away. There was nothing but brutal triumph in Ruan's expression. 'No!'

she cried in dismay. 'You can't, you can't be so cruel! Think of the people we can help! I beg you——'

'Beg? Did I hear you say beg? I thought you'd never do that,' Ruan drawled sardonically.

'Oh, you bastard!' she whispered. 'This is your way of getting your own back on David and me, is it?'

He shrugged with infuriating carelessness. 'It would be quite a blow for you both if the business collapsed, wouldn't it?' he said, his face without expression as if it were carved in granite.

Her hand clutched at her breast where her wildly clamouring heart seemed on the brink of leaping straight out. 'Do you mean you'd make sure the Fondé people heard your disgusting rumours about David's honour? Oh, no,' she groaned. 'You can't be so malicious!'

'Oh, I can. With hardly any effort at all. Caroline *is* a long time, isn't she?' he murmured. 'I think I'd better ring her. Excuse me.'

'Ruan!' She stiffened, suddenly conscious of the time. The woman should have arrived by now. Her eyes flicked up warily. 'I don't want you around,' she grated. 'If I have to, I'll drive you back to Bristol myself.'

'Don't bother,' he said in a lazy voice. 'I said that the balloon had to get back, not me. I can stay if I want to. I'm a free agent. As always. Free as the air.'

'You're not staying here!' she said vehemently.

'I've slept under the stars before.' An amused smile twitched at the curve of his lips. 'With a sweet Cornish mermaid.' She winced. 'I put a ladder against your cottage wall and tapped on your bedroom window,' he continued ruthlessly. 'We watched the moon and you snuggled into my arms.'

'Nothing happened,' she snapped. 'I fell asleep.' And he'd tenderly kissed her and firmly returned her to her virginal bed. She'd cherished that innocent but exciting night for longer than was wise.

'Only because I let you,' he said huskily. 'We both know you were mine for the taking.'

'Ring Caroline!' she ground out.

Tense and agitated, Natasha stayed put to listen to his call, edgily wondering what was going to happen next. Life with Ruan was full of surprises, most of them unpleasant. She sipped her tea, but the liquid didn't ease the terrible parched state of her throat.

'Are you lost or something?' murmured Ruan without preamble, when his call was connected.

She scowled. He seemed to be listening to a long explanation which he greeted with a grunt and finally slammed the phone down without a comment or a goodbye, apparently annoyed. Apparently. Everything he did was under suspicion now.

'Well? What's held her up?' she asked sharply.

'The Land Rover seems to have stopped dead, in the middle of nowhere. She and the crew have decided to sleep in it for the night and come on in the morning.'

It was a blow, but somehow not unexpected. 'What a surprise,' she said caustically. 'Did you arrange this?'

'Of course,' he answered, and she didn't know if he meant that or was teasing her. With a mocking lift of his dark eyebrow, Ruan picked up his flight bag and strode to the door, then paused, his back to her. 'You know,' he mused, 'given a little longer, you could have talked me out of ruining the health clinic.'

'I beg your pardon?!' she gasped.

'You and David smashed my life,' he said quietly. 'I've been planning for some time to do exactly the same to you.'

'Oh, my God!' she whispered.

'However...' He frowned. 'I'm not entirely ruthless. I can see that this clinic could be of benefit to many people. Perhaps you could dissuade me from taking my revenge.' He paused. 'It's well within your powers.'

The door crashed shut behind Ruan's retreating figure and she jumped with the noise. For a few fraught seconds she twisted her fingers in an agony of indecision. Then she ran out into the darkness, to see his tall figure disappearing up the path that led towards the lane.

'Where are you going?' she yelled angrily. 'And what about the balloon?'

'The crew will collect it as soon as they can in the morning,' he called, turning slowly around. 'I have no transport and there are no taxis, so I have no choice but to walk to St Mawes to get a bed.' He remained still for a moment, the two of them facing each other in the chill November night. 'I'll be cold and bad-tempered when I arrive,' he pointed out. 'Less likely to be amenable to the pleas of a beautiful woman.'

'Then you might as well warm yourself up on the way by swigging down that whisky in your bag,' she suggested irritably.

There was a brief silence, as if Ruan had stopped breathing. She remembered with a sinking sensation that she could only have known that his bag carried whisky if she'd searched it. Her heart moved up into second gear, straining in her chest and hammering loudly in her ears. She'd blown it. He'd realise...

'I keep the whisky for farmers or land-owners,' he explained, walking slowly towards her. 'A kind of sweetener, when the balloon fetches up in one of their fields. I was remiss. I should have offered it to you for your hospitality.'

He put the bag down and crouched to undo the straps, his eyes never leaving hers for a second. She had no idea whether he realised she'd betrayed herself or not. Then he frowned, the whisky in his hand. 'Wait a minute; how did you——?'

'Ruan!' she cried hastily, anxious to stop him from putting two and two together. 'I—I do want to persuade you!' He put the bottle back with a slow deliberation as if he was thinking. 'I imagine it would give you great delight if I begged,' she said, grinding the words out grudgingly.

'True.' To her great relief, he forgot the bottle, and turned his attention to her, slowly standing up, an expression of contempt on his handsome face.

It maddened Natasha that she should be going cap in hand to him for a favour. But it was her future—and David's—and he'd been a rock to her. 'OK. I'll crawl if you want me to,' she muttered, 'if it'll stop your vindictive plan to destroy our lives. Please, Ruan. *Please.*'

'Promising start,' he acknowledged laconically. 'Though I care little for your future and less for David's.'

Frantically, she caught his arms, tipping her face to his in a last-ditch plea. 'Please,' she said softly. 'It matters nothing to you. It's everything to us.'

'Kiss me,' he said arrogantly. She closed her eyes, shaking her head in refusal. 'Kiss me,' he growled huskily. The savage passion vibrated into her, and she slowly opened her eyes again to find his face inches away, infinitely kissable. 'Is it that hard?' he whispered.

She gulped, mesmerised by him. If he knew that it was harder to hold back, he'd die of laughter. 'If that's your payment,' she managed, with an indifferent shrug.

Her burning mouth lifted to his. He remained immobile, allowing her to press firmly, a meeting of hot flesh and minimal tenderness. But then his hand clamped around the back of her skull and he was deepening the kiss, crushing her in his arms again, the fierce energy in him exploding in every cell in her brain. Then he let her go. The silence was broken only by their panting—till she deliberately wiped the back of her hand hard across her mouth as if to erase all trace of him.

'Is that enough?' she demanded proudly.

'On the contrary. It's only the beginning,' he said coldly.

'What—what do you mean?' she stammered.

'I think you should stew for a while,' he said, grinding each word out. She gasped, sensing a suppressed violence in him that made her knees weak from fear. 'Beg me all over again, kiss me again, in the morning.'

'But...why not now?' she asked huskily, her voice shaking with emotion. 'I thought we could——'

'No, Natasha,' he said in a soft growl. 'We can't. It's tempting, but that would be too easy and I don't want to make anything easy for you.' He smiled, contemplating her minutely and she felt as if he were a diner in a seafood restaurant selecting live lobster from a tank. 'It's good for you to suffer a little.'

'Why, you——!'

'Careful!' he warned. 'Don't make me angry,' he said with soft savagery. 'I've got you jerking on the end of my line. Wriggle too hard and I'll haul you in, little mermaid.'

'You made me kiss you on false pretences!'

'I made no promises!' he snarled. 'I only demanded and you gave. That's how I like it—me with the power, you running around doing whatever I say. Now I'll take your car so I can drive to St Mawes. That'll make me more responsive to your earnest persuasion tomorrow.'

'You're going to put me through a whole night of worry?' she said, appalled.

'I hope so,' he said smugly.

'You want your pound of flesh!' she accused sullenly.

'I certainly do,' he drawled. 'Maybe,' he continued, looking her up and down meaningfully, 'I *might* decide to be satisfied with exploring your rustic sexual talents for twenty-four hours.'

'Twenty-four *hours*?' she gasped.

'I have a very healthy sexual appetite and a wealth of experience to impart,' he said with soft menace.

'You won't have me!' she said, white-lipped.

'It's a minor punishment, a small sacrifice, when you consider what you owe me in exchange for the ruination of my business and the accusations I had to bear,' he said in deadly lethal tones. 'Does a night and a day of debauchery pay for the despair my mother endured, when we ended up deep in debt because my business failed? When we were shunned by everyone she'd known all her married life?'

'It's happened, it's finished,' she cried piteously.

His eyes glowed like glittering emeralds and his voice became a savage snarl. 'No. It isn't finished till I've taken my revenge in one way or another—till I can close the door on you and David and get on with living my life again.'

'But I didn't mean to hurt you! I loved you!' she wailed.

For a moment it was as if a ghost had crossed his grave. He looked as if he'd seen hell from the inside and never expected to emerge from its dark shadows.

'But not enough,' he growled harshly. 'Imagine what it was like at my home,' he went on relentlessly. 'My father dying. Knowing that I might be sent to prison if the charges of drug smuggling held true. Knowing we could get no credit because of the crippling debt. That David's mother had sacked my mother. That she even had to leave the pub because of the scandal——'

'Ruan, I tried——'

'Shut up!' he roared. 'I haven't finished! We were left with *nothing*—no friends, no work, *nothing*! Not even honour—the most precious thing a Sicilian can possess. All my confidence, my ambitions to create a safe, secure life for my mother were shattered and my father died a sad, disappointed man. Because of you, Natasha Trelawny. Because of you!'

Misting tears half blinding her, she made a helpless gesture of defeat. 'Don't blame me! Everyone was spreading rumours about you,' she blurted out, driven to defend her own overpowering guilt. 'You brought half of London's gangland to St Mawes. You mixed with call-girls—and worse——'

'Who says?' he snarled.

'David! He saw you!' she sobbed. 'I saw some of them, too. They looked shifty——'

'I delivered yachts occasionally,' he said tightly. 'The owners were all kinds—and their women. I sailed their boats across the Channel for them.'

'You met them at night! Isn't that suspicious?'

'Not if that's the only time I had spare,' he growled. 'But you had to believe the gossip, not me.'

'We hardly ever met,' she said miserably. 'You didn't have time for me, day or night. And I went to the parish meeting with David and all I did was to make the mistake of admitting that I'd seen you flashing a light at night to a yacht——'

'And implied I was a drug smuggler,' finished Ruan harshly.

'I didn't imply anything! They kept asking and asking and I only said——'

'You couldn't keep your mouth shut! You didn't think what it would do to me,' he blazed. 'The authorities came down on me like a ton of bricks. I'm lucky I wasn't wrongly imprisoned and that they found no evidence at all of my guilt. And you think a quick, belated apology will amply pay for my suffering. No, Natasha,' he snarled. 'It's not enough. You will suffer. An eye for an eye and a tooth for a tooth. You will feel pain and hardship and you will grovel for mercy. Starting from tomorrow morning.' He flashed her a look of contempt. 'Sleep well,' he growled. 'Next time you might not be alone in bed and if I'm the man with you there'll be no time for you to close your eyes.'

She swayed on her feet, horrified by the virulent hatred he felt for her. It was all out in the open now. His cards were on the table, a hand of aces, and she still dreaded the tricks he had up his sleeve.

'Ruan——' she whispered.

'Get the car keys!' he ordered, with barely leashed fury.

Natasha obediently stumbled inside and returned, silently handing them to him. 'I hate you,' she whispered in a shaking voice. 'I hate you more than anyone I've ever known.'

'Hate me if you must,' he growled, his eyes piercingly green. 'Blow hot and cold, like the fickle wind. But the mere sight of you arouses me to a sexual anger that I've never felt before, and that intrigues and excites me. I'm going to stay around. And I'm going to have your hide, Natasha... One way or another.' He began to walk towards her again and she backed away in terror till she felt the wall of the cottage behind her. 'Nothing will stop me from getting what I want. Declared Goal Challenge,' he said huskily. 'Now that *does* excite me!' he purred.

He stood in front of her, dark and terrifyingly menacing, an animal sexuality pouring from his threatening body. She flattened herself against the unyielding wall, frightened of the damage he might wreak on her.

'You hate me so much that you want to use me and treat me like an object? After all we were to one another——' She broke off with a stifled sob. 'You swine!' she cried jerkily. 'I made one accidental remark——'

'And your embrace with David; was that an accident too?' he rasped, his breath hot on her ice-cold face.

'He was comforting me because I was so miserable that you were a crook! What's happened to you?' she moaned. 'You were single-minded but never vicious——'

'I got walked on,' he said with savage softness. 'And I swore I'd get even—and that no one would ever get the better of me again. Now for another lesson.' His hand gripped her jaw roughly, her eyes pleading with him.

'I don't like you kissing me,' she croaked, seeing by the drowsiness of his eyes what his intention was.

'You will,' he said softly. 'You will learn to need me like a drug that you hate but can't do without.'

'Not if you treat me like one of your London whores!' she whispered.

A flash of fury made his eyes glitter cruelly. 'I think you're wrong,' he muttered. 'I recognise the cause of that dilation of your eyes, the small intake of breath, the frantic beating of your heart——'

'No!' she cried, appalled that her body could be so treacherous.

'——the curling of your toes, the involuntary parting of your lips,' he whispered ruthlessly. 'You're as aroused as I am. Every moment I'm with you, I'm in a state of permanent hunger, and soon that has to be satisfied.'

Natasha forced back the lump that had come up in her throat. 'Not by you,' she croaked defiantly.

'Your face is flushed. I expect your breasts are tingling, aching for my fingers,' he murmured, his dark eyes mocking her guilty gasp. 'Poor, starving Tasha,' he mocked. 'You need me. Why don't you grow up and admit it, instead of pretending to be so mealy-mouthed and prim?'

'David——' she croaked.

'Is not here.' His hand slid between them and curved around the swell of her breast and when she made a little sound of impotent despair in her throat he smiled mockingly. 'That's a start,' he murmured, his fingers suddenly pushing up the jumper and dipping into the cup of her bra.

She jerked when his hand strayed over the naked flesh. 'Don't!' she whispered in dismay.

He smiled at her helplessness. 'Now tell me you don't want me, when your breast lifts to my fingers, when . . .' His eyelids became drowsy with desire and she groaned aloud, her whole body trembling uncontrollably. 'When your nipple hardens even before I touch it and every inch of you screams for my caress, on your breast, your hips, your thighs——'

'Stop it!' she whispered, frantically licking her pale, dry lips. 'Stop this disgusting...'

The words couldn't flow past the harshness of her throat. They lodged in a husky lump, striking her dumb. For Ruan was ruthlessly arousing her and she couldn't prevent her eyes from closing in pleasurable anguish. For several seconds she stood rigidly, transfixed with ecstasy while his thumb and forefinger rotated over the hard, thrusting nipple. All she could hear was his harsh, irregular breathing, all she could see was the image of his dark, sultry face imprinted on her eyelids.

The hand withdrew and she reluctantly opened her eyes, bewildered by what was happening to her. Something in Ruan's eyes made her tense up, and then with a savage movement he bent to brand her with a ruthless, driving kiss that seemed to be demanding her surrender by force alone.

Natasha felt terrified. She'd never known Ruan to be so violent or irrational and she realised he was obsessed with grinding her into the dirt, his Italian blood so far aroused that he could see nothing but vengeance for his wounded dignity. Lust had mingled with his wrath and ungovernable pride. Lust, Wrath, Pride—three of the deadly sins, and he meant her to introduce her to them too, and all the shades between.

Suddenly his pitiless mouth lifted from hers. 'That's the beginning,' he said hoarsely. 'With more to come. I am determined to avenge injustice.' His head lifted proudly. 'In my own inimitable way.'

He turned on his heel and strode to the car. Natasha ran into the cottage, flinging the door shut with a violence that rattled the windows, locking it with nerveless fingers that could hardly hold the key.

Her initial instincts had been right. Ruan was determined to settle an old score. With her legs unable to hold her, she slowly dragged herself up the stairs and flung herself headlong on the bed. He had carried his grudges through all the intervening years since the day he'd been discredited as a businessman and had stormed into her cottage only to discover her in David's arms. She squeezed her eyes tightly but couldn't prevent the helpless tears of remorse, misery, despair...

'Someone help me!' she sobbed. 'Will I ever stop paying for that one dreadful mistake?'

It was a long, endless night. She lay on her bed staring up at the low ceiling, wide awake and afraid. For the second time in her life, Ruan was turning her dreams to ashes, shattering her life and destroying all her self-respect.

That her body should respond to his touch filled her with anguish. It proved to her even more strongly than before that she ought to shun men. A craving for depraved rogues was more than stupid; it was destructive. What a fool she must be!

'Give me strength!' she breathed, dreading the morning.

Incapable of staying in one place and settling, Natasha rose, pulled a jumper over her nightdress and unpacked her belongings. Then she took a long bath in soothing, aromatic oils. In a familiar ritual, she set her china vaporiser so that the sweet, calming perfume of lavender wafted through the room, relaxing the dull ache in her head.

Her sad eyes gazed out at the moonlit creek. The tide was almost up, washing the crescent of sand with a gentle, soothing whisper. The serenity of Penmellin and its old rhythms flowed into her, giving her the strength she needed and reminding her with a sudden start that she was only really happy in Cornwall. She wanted to stay here among the people she'd grown up with and she wanted to help people who needed her skills. And no vengeful Sicilian was going to stop her.

'It's war,' she said aloud, her eyes as dark as the murmuring water, vowing to fight the injustice of Ruan's vengeance. 'No holds barred.'

War. With an unorthodox schemer like Ruan, she'd have to fight dirty sometimes. She shuddered, but comforted herself as she slid into bed that the stakes were high and she had everything to lose.

'Ruan! Ruan! Answer the door!'

Natasha sat bolt upright to find sunlight dancing on the Percuil river and someone hammering furiously on the plank doors with his or her bare fists.

'Wait a minute!' she yelled.

Muzzy from sleep, she stumbled over to the window, knowing at first sight that this must be the elusive Caroline. If it was, she thought, shot through with unreasonable jealousy, she was gorgeous. The woman's gazelle legs disappeared into a minute Lycra skirt and she had the hair and a body to rival Marilyn Monroe's.

'Who the heck are you?' scowled Caroline. She examined Natasha's tumbled hair and demure nightdress then folded her arms ominously over her lush breasts.

'It doesn't matter. Ruan's not here. He's staying in St Mawes,' answered Natasha, pushing down a rush of violent jealousy and trying not to wonder if Ruan had ever whispered passionately in the ear of the woman beneath the window.

'Oh, really?' said Caroline, plainly not believing her.

Natasha heaved a sigh and frowned at the two men sitting in a dusty Land Rover. 'Are they here to move this thing off the beach?' she asked with relief. 'Wait a minute. I'll come down.'

On the landing, she paused, smelling the unmistakable aroma of bacon and eggs. An awful suspicion crossed her mind.

'Don't hover up there, Tash,' came Ruan's complaining voice from below. 'Answer the door. I've got my hands full.'

Her eyes blazing into life, she thundered down to discover Ruan standing in front of a frying-pan, the big stretch of his naked back to her, and what she could see of his bent head was slicked with black curls as if he'd just emerged from a shower. Only she didn't have one.

'What are you doing in my kitchen and how did you get in?' she grated, on her way to the door.

'Cooking breakfast and through the window,' he answered, concentrating on the delicate operation of flipping over an egg.

'It wasn't open.'

'I'm a master of breaking and entering.' He frowned, carefully basting eggs, his tongue-tip pinkly protruding from his mouth in concentration as he tried to keep the fat from spitting at his naked chest. 'Hearts and windows.'

She bit back her temper at waking and being confronted with a half-nude invader and lifted the bar across the door. This must be part of his scheme to rattle her.

'If you want Ruan, he's here and you're welcome to him. Take him away,' she said curtly to the impatiently waiting woman.

'My, oh, my,' said Caroline sarcastically, sweeping in, a flurry of expensive perfume wafting into the room. 'You don't waste any time, do you?'

'You can't, with eggs,' said the engrossed Ruan.

Caroline gave Natasha the once-over. 'You said she was plain.'

'Isn't she?'

'With that hair and that face?' scoffed Caroline, while Natasha went crimson with embarrassment and humiliation. 'I knew you had the reputation of being a cold-blooded rat, darling,' she said to Ruan, 'but I didn't think you'd take advantage of a simple village girl——'

'Wait a minute!' cried Natasha indignantly. 'He didn't take advantage of me and I'm not simple!'

Caroline's icy blue eyes flipped up and down the tumble-haired Natasha, and the demure, high-necked nightdress. 'Any woman who wears winceyette with a man like Ruan around is simple,' she said scornfully.

'But warm,' retorted Ruan. 'And less obvious, don't you think? And it's got a wildly soft texture that invites exploration.'

'Well! Now I know where I stand,' snapped Caroline. 'It's perfectly clear that I'm not wanted here.'

Natasha saw that Ruan was dreamily pushing bacon around in the pan, a smile of deep contentment on his face. She had to admit that he looked as if he'd swallowed cat, cream, dish and all. 'You calculating rat-fink!' she said coldly. Ruan grinned and turned the mushrooms. 'Caroline——'

'Oh, don't apologise,' she said, waving an arm in dismissal. 'I've got other fish to fry.'

'Oh, I get it,' said Natasha, suddenly realising what he was up to. 'You've set this up! You have a witness now so that you can blacken my name, to make it seem as if I'm immoral—and perhaps unsuitable for my job——'

'Wrong,' he said calmly, ladling all the food on to one plate. 'Got any pepper?'

'If I had, I'd throw it in your face,' she snapped. 'Caroline, the whole thing's been staged. I suggest you search my bedroom and try to find evidence that Ruan slept with me last night——'

'I doubt he'd bother to use a bed,' Caroline said drily. She put her hands on the table and leaned over, eyeing sardonically the unconcerned Ruan, who was happily munching crispy bacon. 'I met an old friend of yours last night.'

'Really? Do I have any around here?' he asked absently.

'David Veane,' answered Caroline. 'He found us by the roadside last night. I persuaded him to take us back to his home. We got chatting and had a few drinks. Nice man.'

'Filthy rich,' said Ruan, watching her closely.

Caroline beamed and affectionately pushed back Ruan's wet curls from his forehead, making Natasha's hands clench at the proprietorial way she did it. 'I'm meeting up with him again when we've taken the balloon back. You don't mind, do you?'

'Not at all; you have a lot in common.' He smiled indulgently. 'Will you tell him about Natasha and me being here? With her in her nightdress and me freshly scrubbed, pleasantly satisfied with life and cooking breakfast?'

'No! She won't—will you? It's all a mistake!' cried Natasha hoarsely, horrified how the truth could be twisted.

'Funny how people can jump to conclusions,' observed Ruan in a mocking drawl.

'What's that supposed to mean?' Natasha snapped.

His eyes glinted from under the line of his dark brows. 'That mistakes can be made about someone's reputation. Sexual and professional.'

She stared at him. Appalled, she was certain now why he'd staged this scene, knowing that Caroline was about to arrive. 'This is my lesson, is it?' she said tightly.

'Reputations can be broken by careless, casual remarks.' Ruan's expression was chilling.

'"Judge not, that ye be not judged".'

'Something like that.'

'I knew it!' she seethed.

They stared at one another for a few heated seconds, Natasha's eyes showing her distress, Ruan's a relentless determination.

'My goodness,' came Caroline's surprised voice. 'You two certainly are crazy about each other, aren't you?'

Natasha looked at her in amazement but there was no mockery in her eyes, only a wistful envy.

'Stick to the script, Caroline,' muttered Ruan. 'And pack the balloon up. I'll be out in a while to check it.'

Caroline laughed. 'I'd never have believed it,' she murmured, her eyes amused. 'Shame,' she sighed. 'I'd almost got it made. Ah, well, I'll leave you to say goodbye in private.' Ruan scowled after her departing back.

'I think you've lost that fish,' said Natasha, grimly pleased.

"I think you've probably lost yours, too,' he said curtly.

'What do you mean?'

'David. You thought you'd landed him, gasping on the bank, didn't you? He doesn't know it yet, but he'll fall prey to another cold-blooded angler who's far more adept at getting her hooks into men. Without your meal ticket, what will you do?'

She smiled to herself. It didn't matter if David and Caroline became friends or lovers. She didn't care at all. Ruan had no idea about the truth of the situation. 'He'll never abandon me,' she said confidently.

'He's abandoned all the usual principles, why not you?' Ruan retorted. 'I think second-hand goods stand low on his list of acquisitions.'

'He won't think for a minute that we slept together last night,' she said haughtily.

'Depends how many people tell him we did,' countered Ruan with unnerving assurance.

'He knows me. You imagine that you can come between us,' she said defiantly, 'but our friendship and affection have never wavered. I trust him and he trusts me. Excuse me. I must dress.'

With a rigid spine and head held high, she walked stiffly up the stairs. It was obvious that she had to speak to David quickly and make the situation clear before Caroline or anyone else poisoned his mind. Ruan had been right about one thing: appearances could be deceptive.

Uncertain who might be at the clinic, she decided to opt for something smart and understated. She swept up her hair and piled it neatly on top of her head, allowing only a few strands to escape and soften the effect. When she came down wearing a tailored charcoal skirt and cream blouse, with a long, elegant jacket, Ruan was still there, checking through his maps.

He let out a low whistle. 'Classy,' he murmured.

She ignored him and made to walk out, longing to put some distance between herself and the devious Ruan. But he stepped in front of her, the mass of his bare, muscular chest barring the way. So she stared coldly at his strong throat, immune, for once, to the warm flesh inches from her breasts.

'David is coming,' she reminded him haughtily. 'I'm waiting outside for him. Move away. He'll be here soon, I expect.'

'Not if Caroline sways her hips and does the boop-a-doop at him first,' Ruan drawled.

Her anger-laden eyes flashed up to his. 'You find this very amusing, playing with people's emotions, don't you?' she said scornfully. 'And to think I once imagined you had a heart packed away in that artfully tanned chest of yours! Let me pass. You've tried to compromise me and make me look cheap in David's eyes, so be satisfied with that. There's no one here now to witness anything else you might consider doing.'

'With your hair up and your war-paint on, you look utterly invincible,' he murmured, and from the way he was contemplating her, touching his lips with the tip of his tongue, she knew with a sinking feeling that she'd offered him a challenge he meant to accept. 'Do I take it, then, that you don't mean to plead for my mercy this morning?'

'Do I hell!' she said proudly, meeting his calculating gaze with defiance.

'Oh, dear,' he said, with infinite regret. 'Don't you know that the more you resist me, the more I feel compelled to bring you to heel?'

'I'm a woman, not a dog!'

'Not even a bitch?'

'Get out of my way,' she said in a low tone. 'I don't want to breathe the same air as you. I'm going to wait for David and I mean to warn him that you're out to ruin us both. By the time I've finished explaining everything, he won't believe a word you say. He's known me all my life. He knows I'm too decent to let a man like you touch me. Leave my house! I don't want you in it!'

Ruan smiled faintly and reached for his jacket, his muscles rippling as he eased into it and slowly inched up the zip. 'My goodness, you're angry! You don't have a hope in hell against me,' he said softly. 'Not while there's all that pent-up frustration inside you. What will you do if David succumbs to Caroline's obvious charms and there's no man to warm your bed? Your sexual hunger will cloud your judgement——'

'It won't! David's never made love to me!' she yelled, incensed. Her mouth shut tightly in dismay.

'Good lord!' drawled Ruan in amusement. 'My instincts were right. He's been kept at arm's length. You know,' he said in a confidential tone, 'one day you'll have to reward him for his patience.'

'I intend to. He deserves my admiration and affection,' she said, lifting her chin stubbornly.

Ruan's lip curled. 'And you both deserve what I have in store for you,' he said softly. 'Remember, Natasha. I shall have you.' Arrogantly confident, he strolled out, leaving her feeling agitated and filled with a sense of foreboding.

CHAPTER FIVE

NATASHA killed time by clearing the kitchen of the debris Ruan had left from cooking his breakfast. She refused to look out of the window at the activity outside, but eventually heard the Land Rover drive away, returning Penmellin to its dreaming silence.

She waited, and waited. And waited. Her shoulders began to slump. Surely David couldn't have forgotten her? After an hour and a half, and fruitless telephone calls to the nursing home—where she discovered that his new home number was ex-directory—she heard the sound of a car, bumping along the track. Smiling with relief that he'd had only been delayed after all, she hurried out eagerly.

Her face fell when she saw it was Ruan, lounging in an open-top car that gleamed glossy black and slunk long and low towards her and purred like a contented tiger. She frowned. He'd changed his clothes, and now wore a dark navy suit with a fine stripe that curved over his big chest and shoulders in such a perfect fit that even at this distance she knew it must have cost serious money.

'New Jag. Like it?' he yelled as he drew up outside the cottage door. His audacious grin matched the bright white wedge of his shirt.

'Impractical,' she replied frostily, stopping her eyes from admiring its sleek, wickedly sensual lines. 'You'd be better off with a four-wheel-drive down here.'

'I like to run more than one model,' he said with a laugh.

'Yes, you would,' she muttered, glowering at him.

Only his hair, appealingly tousled by the wind, was at odds with her startling impression of an impeccably dressed and extremely wealthy man. His arm hung casually over the gleaming door, a heavy signet-ring and a massive gold watch catching the sun's rays, winking in unison with the gold pin in his scarlet tie.

'David stood you up?'

Her mouth firmed. 'I expect he's been delayed,' she answered frigidly.

'Yes,' he sighed. 'I dropped Caroline at his front gate on the way out. She seemed keen to get closely acquainted.'

'You know where he lives?' she asked in astonishment. 'Tell me!'

He leaned over and opened the passenger door. 'Better than that, Tash,' he said cheerfully. 'I'll take you there.'

'Why?' she asked coldly.

'Don't look a gift horse in the mouth,' he murmured.

'I have. Its teeth are rotten,' she snapped.

'But it doesn't travel on its teeth and it knows the way, so who cares?' he grinned. 'Ride off with me into the unknown and save David from the jaws of the monster. I'm sure it bothers you that your rich boyfriend is being swept off by a rapacious dragon.'

Natasha frowned at the description of Caroline. She faced him with total composure, her hands casually in the pockets of her flattering jacket, one high-heeled shoe neatly positioned in front of the other. Cool, contained, sophisticated. She could handle him. She had to.

'Where is he?'

'You want to know, you come with me,' Ruan insisted.

'You could be abducting me,' she said coldly.

'I could.'

She glared. 'You could be lying.'

'Life is one long risk, isn't it?' he drawled.

She weighed the options. 'I suppose I'll have to take that risk,' she said crossly. 'But touch me just once on the journey and I'll have you before the courts for assault!'

'I love it when you talk tough,' he teased.

Natasha gritted her teeth and stalked towards the car, aware that there had been a flash of triumph in his eyes, and it set her mind on full alert. Ruan was plotting something again.

'Wherever did you hire this car?' she asked curiously, marvelling at the heavy clunk of the door and the body-caressing comfort of the soft leather seat. 'It's hardly the standard heap you can normally rent out.'

Ruan wasn't listening. He was gazing out at the glistening strand, a sunlit, golden, wet crescent, in-habited now by piping oyster-catchers. His eyes fol-lowed the arrow-flight of two cormorants, skimming close to the crystal-clear water, and she sensed a wist-fulness in the slight angle of his dark head. Slowly he scanned the cove, to where salt marsh met the beach and the lichened branches of ancient oak and beech trees hung low over the retreating tidal flat.

He sighed as if the hauntingly beautiful scene affected even his stony heart. 'Is the spring still flowing?' he asked suddenly.

'I don't know.' She thought of the natural spring that emerged from the rock-face where they'd washed their muddy feet one day and she desperately tried to think of something else because all she could see in her mind's eye now was his heart-stopping kiss on the arching sole of her foot.

'Got to find out.' Ruan was out of the car and striding along to the rock-face behind the fish cellars before she could blink. Curiosity made her follow, an aching need to touch base, to reassure herself that her old familiar haunts had not changed, even if Ruan had.

'It's a mercy that some things remain constant,' she observed sourly, seeing Ruan sipping the sparkling fresh water.

He pressed his hand against the encrusted moss and dainty navelwort, his face quite transformed. 'It tastes . . . different,' he said softly.

'It's not polluted, is it?' she cried in dismay, stepping forward awkwardly on her spiky heels to investigate. Her head bent and she felt the icy trickle of water touch her lips. 'Nectar,' she pronounced in relief. 'Perhaps your tastes have changed.' Her eyes flickered. He was looking at her moist mouth longingly.

'I wish they had,' he said heavily. 'I wish to God they had.'

Abruptly he strode away, leaving Natasha mystified. He revved the engine loudly, sending the alarmed oyster-catchers soaring upwards and wheeling over the cove.

They drove up the side of the wooded valley, looking down on the winding river which ran to Tredinnick. But when they came to the crossroads, instead of turning towards the lane which would take them to the King Harry ferry and then on to Falmouth, he took the narrow road which led down to Tredinnick House itself.

'Wait a minute,' she said, grabbing his arm tightly. 'You're going in the wrong direction.' Impatiently she tucked back her wind-swept hair. 'Don't try to play clever! I know my way around, remember? If you're trying——'

He shook her off. 'How could I forget that we both know this area better, perhaps, than we know each other?' he muttered. 'I'm taking you to David, as I said.'

'At Tredinnick?' she ridiculed.

'Yes.'

Her hand fell away. He meant it. And he was very, very angry, the bones of his face standing out with tension, the set of his jaw hard as if he was desperately trying to control a volcanic fury that had been leashed for too long.

'David is waiting *there*? Why?' she frowned.

Low sun began to flash intermittently through the bare branches of the hedge. Ruan pushed on a pair of dark glasses which hid his eyes and emphasised the fact that he had changed from the man she'd known to a sexy, mysterious stranger. He angrily pushed the button on the tape deck. Music began to play, harsh, wild music that seemed to echo Ruan's mood and set Natasha's teeth on edge.

'Because he owns Tredinnick,' he shouted over the blast of sound.

'Owns it?' Stunned, Natasha sat back to think—as far as she could, with such violent music assaulting her ears.

The lane ran deep below the Cornish hedges formed by dry-stone walls topped by centuries of earth, by thorn, ash and wild rose, brambles and honeysuckle. She glanced at Ruan again for clarification as he slowly negotiated its dangerous blind corners. As always, he drove with a serious concentration, and once she'd imagined that had been to keep her safe. Now she knew better. He only cared for his own skin.

His mouth betrayed his feelings, working in anger. And slowly she began to appreciate the extent of his bitterness. 'My reaction was somewhat stronger when I heard,' he rasped. 'Don't tell me you didn't know.'

She stared ahead again at the winding lane, shielding her eyes from the flickering sun. 'No, I didn't—if it's true. What makes you think it is?'

'They confirmed it at the post office.'

'You sound as if you'd had wind of this before,' she said shrewdly.

He turned down the music. 'That's why I came.'

'I see.' Now it was clear. 'You'd heard a rumour from somewhere and couldn't bear the thought that David had acquired the house you'd set your heart on as a small child,' she accused. 'I had no idea you two were so competitive.'

'I was just me,' he said shortly. 'David competed.'

'You envy him,' she said, mentally ticking off yet another of Ruan's sins. 'And I know why.'

His head jerked in her direction and then back again, his profile grim. 'Oh? Tell me,' he snapped.

'Tredinnick represented something special, something good in your past before you were corrupted. It was the house that had listened to all your ambitions, all your hopes and dreams,' she said in a low voice.

'And you. You're in my past and you heard them too,' he said harshly. 'I shared my dreams with you.'

Something made her want to hurt him. 'I also heard you swear to love me forever,' she said sarcastically— though she shook with unseen misery. 'But that didn't last long, did it?'

His breath exhaled noisily. 'How you've changed,' he growled.

Life had soured them both, she thought sadly. It didn't seem long ago that she and Ruan were playing in Tredinnick's tangled and overgrown subtropical gardens, thrilled with their secret world. They'd walked, talked, planned, tussled, laughed, argued...and always regarded Tredinnick as theirs. All three of them had boasted they'd own it one day. Her heart ached to know that the starry-eyed, madly ambitious Ruan had become cynical and hard.

'I'm sure you're mistaken about David owning Tredinnick,' she began.

'I'd like to think so. But I know he does.'

'Oh, come on, Ruan! Even as dilapidated as it is, it must be worth a fortune! An Elizabethan manor house with a Georgian façade and an overgrown botanist's garden that runs down to the sea? That alone would make the estate an expensive proposition. Do you remember the maze, and those tree ferns? The stands of bamboo and the weird giant rhubarb we sheltered under, with leaves as big as your kitchen table?'

'Gunnera,' he said tightly. 'It's called gunnera.'

'Well, whatever,' she said impatiently, faintly surprised that he could name the plant. 'David doesn't have that kind of money.'

'He *didn't*,' Ruan said meaningfully. 'He still doesn't, for that matter,' he added with an ironic curl to his lip.

'How could he buy it, then?' she asked, baffled. 'Has he got out a loan from the bank? Borrowed cash?'

Ruan laughed unpleasantly. 'In a manner of speaking.'

He sounded very certain of his facts and Natasha wondered how he knew so much. 'It would have to be an enormous amount,' she said anxiously. 'I hope he hasn't double-mortgaged his nursing home.'

'He's not that stupid. It's the goose that lays his golden eggs.' He shot her a quick glance. 'Either you're a very good liar, or he's kept you in the dark. Don't you realise that he's setting up his health clinic in Tredinnick itself?'

An incredulous smile transformed her worried expression to one of joy. 'Really? Can that be true? Our childhood fantasy-house? Oh, Ruan, think how heavenly it would be to live and work there!'

The blank black sunglasses met her grey-blue gaze, reflecting the wind-swept hair streaming back from her eager face. 'Clever, clever David,' he muttered. 'I underestimated him. He's hooked you by using exactly the right bait.'

'David doesn't operate like you,' she said coldly. 'He's far more caring and hasn't a calculating bone in his body.'

Ruan smiled tightly but made no reply. They had come to the huge old lodge gates, once rusted and broken-hinged, now restored with black paint gleaming on the fancy ironwork. Excited, Natasha jumped out of the car and opened them, discovering that they swung easily as if they'd been carefully oiled.

The massed rhododendrons along the sweeping drive had been tamed and the grass scythed down and now it neatly edged the gravel. Someone had put a lot of work into the once wild garden.

'Can he really have bought Tredinnick?' she breathed, still not daring to believe it. 'The upkeep alone—oh, Ruan!'

He had stopped the car where the avenue of great chestnuts opened to give a view of the house. 'My God!' he breathed in shocked awe. 'He's got in some good people to work on the renovations. It's absolutely wonderful!'

Natasha was equally amazed at the transformation. 'Breathtaking! It's been totally renovated! You must be right!' she cried in glee. Her mind ticked over, estimating the likely cost. 'He must have found an extremely generous backer,' she said, voicing her thoughts as her wide eyes scanned the huge house.

'Or a bottomless pit.'

She ignored his sarcasm. 'I'm amazed he ever discovered who owned it. I thought that was a mystery.'

'Not to me. It's surprising what you can find out if you know the right people,' he said drily.

'OK, whose was it?'

'To begin with, it was part of the demesne of Sir Walter Raleigh. You know he owned a lot of land around here. He gifted it to the squire of Tredinnick—for services rendered in the Spanish Main. A Tredinnick descendant owned it till David moved in,' replied Ruan. 'A motley bunch of owners.'

'What do you mean?' she asked waspishly.

His eyebrow lifted mockingly. 'Raleigh was, when all's said and done, a ruthless pirate-lord. The Tredinnicks were a family who got rich by exploiting Cornwall's tin miners. And finally,' he sneered, 'carrying on a long line of brutal villains, there's our own home-grown bastard. David.'

His comments were so derogatory that they weren't worth attention. Calling David a brutal villain was ridiculous. Natasha set her teeth, determined to pass on the news that Ruan was out to spread muck. Acres of it. She had to move fast, if she was to keep ahead of the slander. There was so much more to lose now, she thought soberly. The most beautiful house in Cornwall.

Yet despite her anxiety she couldn't help but smile at the sight of the house she loved, looking so handsome and well cared for. No wonder David hadn't wanted Ruan to discover what had happened to Tredinnick! He knew how possessive and jealous Ruan would be.

The car slid to a halt in front of the grand stone steps. Forgetting everything but the thought of spending her days at Tredinnick, Natasha was hugging herself with delight. She leapt eagerly out of the car and ran up to wait beneath the pillared portico while the sounds of a sonorous bell echoed behind the massive door.

'David! Hello! Isn't this exciting?' she cried eagerly when he opened the door.

'Oh! Natasha!' David looked rather disconcerted. And rather ruffled, she thought, his shirt oddly buttoned, his tie askew. 'I—er—got delayed. I was going to come for you after coffee but——'

'Never mind, I'm here now,' she smiled happily, stepping inside. 'You are an old sly-boots! You never told me you lived here! Why keep it such a secret? You know how much I love this place——'

'Get rid of Ruan,' frowned David, interrupting. 'What did you bring him for?'

'He brought me. I didn't know where you'd got to, remember?' she reminded him gently.

The telephone rang and then stopped before he could reach it. Natasha smiled to placate the agitated David and tucked her arm in his, gazing around at the chequer-floored hall which had been decorated in exquisite country-house taste, a roaring log fire in the corner and comfortable chintzy armchairs grouped invitingly around.

'I'm slowly prising information out of him,' she said quietly to him. 'He's doing his best to cause trouble. He's already upset his girlfriend, who thinks I spent the night with him. But it's not true, David. I loathe the man. You know I do. Don't believe him. I'm loyal to you, through and through.'

'Ah,' came Ruan's silken voice from behind her left shoulder. 'But is he loyal to you?'

They all looked up to see Caroline walking—no, swaying—slowly down the double staircase, one hand lightly on the mahogany banister carved with dragon's scales. Natasha felt Ruan's breath on her neck and wondered if he too had a vivid memory of sliding down the banisters, he on the left, she on the right, to grapple with the twin dragons' heads which reared up menacingly at each other.

'I took your phone call, David,' said Caroline casually. 'The line was awful, but there's Paris for you. Someone called Fondy is coming this morning——'

'*Fondé*?' yelled David. 'Did you say...? Oh, my God! We're not ready! Tell me the message properly,' he demanded urgently.

'She was foreign but I think she said it was Fondy,' Caroline shrugged, 'and that the Proprytair or something was coming to interview a Miss Trelawny.'

'*Le propriétaire*,' murmured Ruan. 'The owner. My goodness, you are honoured. The owner! You must be petrified at the thought. It's such an important matter. I'd be devastated—I mean, you're not expecting him, are you? Tasha's only just arrived——'

'All right,' said Natasha irritably. 'Stop going on about it. I can cope with an interview.'

'Do you want an interpreter?' he offered, all innocence. 'I can *parler* a bit. If he speaks only French, you'll have a few communication problems.'

'Ruan, you're not hanging around to throw a spanner in the works. Get out of here,' said David with dignity.

'And don't even think of felling a tree across the drive, or putting tacks down to damage the man's car——'

'What a devious mind you've developed,' marvelled Ruan. 'I'd never have thought of those things. I swear that I won't harm a hair of this man's head or annoy him in any way.'

Natasha was worried. Ruan seemed highly pleased with himself, charged with energy like a dynamo. 'OK, his head's safe, but would you harm any other part of him?' she asked suspiciously.

He laughed in delight. 'At last you've learnt to think less sloppily than before!' he chuckled. 'No, Tash. My solemn vow on it. I would go so far as to say that I'd go to great lengths to make sure he never comes to any harm.'

'Thank God!' muttered David. 'OK. Push off, Ruan. We've got to get our skates on, Natasha. Er—Caroline, can we settle that matter quickly?' he asked, reddening up at Natasha's look of astonishment. 'I'll be with you in a moment,' he told her. 'I've got an arrangement to make first. Keep an eye out for this guy and give me a shout if he comes before I return.'

'What's his name?' she asked in agitation.

'Don't know. I've always dealt with the franchise manager. I'll find the letter-head. I won't be long,' he assured her.

'You all but threw them together,' Natasha said accusingly to Ruan, as David hurried off with Caroline. 'I'm beginning to wonder if you had a hidden motive.'

'Perhaps I was bored with her,' he murmured.

'You bastard!' she gasped.

He lowered his voice. 'Don't tell David. Think what it'll do to his self-esteem if he discovers she gave up trying to land me and decided to take second best.'

'You are a smug, self-satisfied, egocentric chauvinist,' she said coldly.

'And you don't have a rich boyfriend any more.'

She gave him a superior smile, deciding to smash his illusions. 'You've wasted your energies, Ruan,' she said in glacial tones. 'David never was my boyfriend and I don't care whom he goes around with. I'm here for the job he's offered.'

'No love, only commercial gain, then?' he asked lightly.

'My work has become more important to me than the fickle emotions of men,' she answered serenely. 'Excuse me. I think I'd better find out where everything is if I'm to receive this man.'

'You've forgotten something,' he said menacingly. 'Your future is in my hands.' She stopped in mid-stride and he caught her up, pulling her back and whirling her around so roughly that she nearly lost her balance. 'I wonder if this man from your cosmetics company would be interested in the loose morals of David and yourself?' he growled.

'No!' she whispered, opening her dusky blue eyes in alarm. 'You won't sabotage my interview——'

'Won't I?' he murmured with a cruel smile.

For a moment she stared at him in dismay, her legs weak with nerves. 'Do you intend to tell him lies about me?' she demanded shakily.

'Not lies,' corrected Ruan, smoothing his hand over his wind-blown hair till it lay sleek. He suddenly looked every inch a businessman and Natasha knew he'd cut an impressive and convincing figure if he confronted Fondé's owner. A quiver of apprehension ran through her. 'He ought to know the kind of woman who's representing his impeccable products, though, don't you think?'

She felt sick. It was the beginning of his plan to make her suffer. 'You didn't seduce me last night! I'm innocent, you know that!' she cried.

'I do. But does Caroline? Did she tell David? Perhaps that's why he looked so embarrassed when you turned up on his doorstep. Or...maybe I told the people in the post office this morning.' He smiled at her appalled expression.

She took a deep, shuddering breath. 'You opportunist! You realised that even if you didn't manage to seduce me you could pretend that you had!'

'You see how easy it is to condemn someone,' he purred. 'A hint here, a compromising little kiss there...'

'You don't even pretend to deny it! You are evil!' she whispered.

'When I have to be,' he answered quietly. 'You realise that if this man doesn't approve of you, then any plans to develop Tredinnick as a health centre can be forgotten.'

'But David has probably borrowed an enormous amount of money!' she cried in horror.

'On the strength of Fondé's reputation?' smiled Ruan smugly. 'Oh, dear! He could be in terrible trouble if the franchise fell through. They might call in the debt. I could almost sympathise with that situation,' he continued in a hard tone. 'I remember how devastating that was myself.'

Waves of nausea scoured her stomach. His revenge, an eye for an eye and a tooth for a tooth, was being played out exactly as he had planned. He had lost his business; he was doing his darnedest to make sure David did too—and that she suffered the consequences.

'They won't believe you! I'll explain... Please, Ruan, stop hounding us!' she moaned, her eyes bright with angry tears. 'You've done enough damage, you've made me suffer enough——'

'Not in my opinion,' he said harshly. 'You've a long way to go yet. I haven't even begun to twist the knife.'

'Haven't you? Don't you know what you did to me when we quarrelled?' she whispered. 'I cried endlessly when I found out how hollow you were, because you'd been my whole world! I cried till my face was swollen and ugly and I couldn't eat because I couldn't even swallow. My hair fell out!' she wailed piteously. 'In handfuls! You bastard, I've suffered—— Oh, God, how I've suffered! And all because I was crazy enough to have loved you and trusted all my heart to you!'

Ruan seemed turned to stone. But his eyes burned with a black fire that frightened her. 'Tash——' he began, in a strange, choked voice.

'I have to get ready to meet this guy,' she said to him in a shaking voice, trying to get her priorities straight. 'You're attempting to confuse me, to——'

'Will you spend the night with me in exchange for my promise to keep my mouth shut?' enquired Ruan, as casually as if he were asking her to join him in a knitting circle.

'I will not!' she yelled, aghast. 'That's the most immoral suggestion I've ever heard!'

'Well, now,' said Ruan speculatively. 'Either sex with me is totally repellent, or your job isn't as important as you said it was——'

'Or I don't do deals with my body and I don't believe you'd keep your promise,' she grated.

'Don't you wish you'd never come back, Natasha?' he asked huskily. 'Would you like me to drive you to the station, so that you can put this whole unpleasant business behind you?'

She took a long, oxygenating breath. Ruan can't reach me, she told herself. People will take one look at his knowing face and mine and know whom to believe. I will win this battle.

'I intend to live here,' she said levelly. 'I intend to help David make this marvellous enterprise a resounding success and I will convince this Fondé guy and anyone else you try to corrupt with your lies that David and I are honest, innocent of any crime you try to smear us with, and highly moral.' Her head lifted high on the pale column of her neck and she met Ruan's eyes with her own challenge.

'Better get rid of Caroline, then,' he said with an infuriating smile. 'She's never heard of the word platonic.'

'Just go,' said Natasha coldly. 'And don't stop if you meet anyone on the way out.'

'I doubt that I will,' Ruan said, oddly in command of the situation despite her brave stand against him. 'Because I'm not leaving. I'll be staying here a few weeks.'

'Then I'll have to call the police,' she said angrily.

'I wouldn't do that if I were you,' he murmured. 'David would have a heart attack. Besides, you don't want to upset such an important man, do you?' The smug assurance in his voice stopped her from making a sharp retort. He slipped a hand into his breast pocket and brought out a slim leather case, opening it and waving it in front of Natasha's nose. She backed away haughtily. 'Read,' he commanded in a menacing voice laden with triumph.

His passport was tucked in one side. In the other...a gold card. The letters danced before her eyes but already the words were imprinted on her brain.

'"Ruan Gardini. *Le Propriétaire*, Fondé"!' she frowned. 'Oh, very amusing!' she said scathingly. 'How did you make this forgery?' Her contemptuous eyes examined the identification card with Ruan's unmistakably arrogant signature. And the address in Paris, a telephone number, a fax number...

'I never quite mastered forgery,' he admitted ruefully.

'You had it specially printed.'

'Sure? No doubts creeping in?' he drawled. 'Just take a good look at me, Natasha. The suit. French. The shoes. French. The shirt, ditto. Ah. I see you can judge quality hand-tailoring when you see it. Recall my leather gear? Was that expensive or not? You should know, you handled it enough——'

'I—I——' she floundered. It couldn't be true. He might be a salesman for the conglomerate or——

'Ring them,' he suggested maliciously.

Her eyes blazed. 'I will!' She used the telephone number from her own letter in her handbag, but it was the same as Ruan's. And the girl on the switchboard confirmed that the owner of Fondé was a Monsieur Ruan Gardini.

Her nerveless fingers dropped the receiver, which Ruan caught with his customary dexterity and replaced. Taking the letter from her, he pointed out the name in small type below the masthead. 'Ruan Gardini, *Propriétaire*.' Her eyes closed. It was unbelievable, but it was true. They were finished.

'How...?' The words stuck in her throat.

'Nice trick?' murmured Ruan.

Miserably she lifted her lashes to gaze at him with moist eyes. 'You hold all the cards,' she admitted in a low tone.

'Cards?' he said, with a cynical lift of his dark eyebrows. 'I own the whole damn gambling den. That means I control who wins and who loses, and guess whose side I'm on?'

'Oh, no!' she groaned.

She was in danger of losing what she'd had almost within her grasp: a secure future, a wonderful job, companionship with David and the pleasure of working in Tredinnick House. A short while ago she had only to reach out and touch it and it would have been hers. Now it was probably lost forever.

'I've been associated with Fondé for some time.' Ruan smiled coldly at her uplifted white face. 'I began by organising and leading their research parties into jungles. So, you see, we did meet, after all, and we all got on like a house on fire. A kind of mutual respect grew up between us.'

'They respected you?' she repeated stupidly.

'Hard to believe, isn't it?' he drawled. 'But I'd been in Bolivia making my fortune in the oil business and had travelled extensively in South America. I knew it well, flora and fauna, that sort of thing.' He smiled faintly. 'I photographed the parrots, incidentally. Anyway, I liked the Fondé men immediately; they liked me. When old man Fondé died, it seemed a good business to invest my money in. I made them an offer they couldn't refuse—as I always do. A massive take-over bid.'

'Natasha!' yelled David, running back into the hall, his expression horror-struck.

'I know!' she shouted. 'I know who he is!'

'Oh, God!' David groaned. 'For God's sake, if it's true, I'll be ruined! I'll lose everything!'

'Like to be certain of my credentials? Caroline!' Ruan commanded. 'Get my briefcase.'

'She knew,' rasped Natasha. 'She works for you, but she pretended not to know who had telephoned——'

'Don't blame her,' said Ruan quietly. 'She was only following instructions. I made sure she knew that her job was on the line if she didn't do as she was told.'

'You bastard!' breathed David. 'That defenceless woman, blackmailed by you!'

Ruan's dark eyebrow shot up in disbelief, but he controlled his wavering mouth hastily. And, as if to allay any vestige of doubt, he began to list the details of David's negotiation with Fondé. Natasha realised he knew them by heart. He listed the products one by one. When his briefcase arrived, he snapped open the locks and passed copies of the correspondence to David to peruse.

'No doubts?' he murmured. 'You must admit I'd find it hard to bribe the whole Fondé switchboard or to replicate the letter-head *and* to steal the necessary documentation.'

'I don't understand,' muttered Natasha. 'You, an entrepreneur? A businessman? When did you get the time? Not long ago you were playing around with women on rafts, piloting them down the Zambesi——'

'Pure fun,' he said casually. 'I played hookey. Boardrooms get claustrophobic.'

'But... you're not the sort of man to fit in with a company like this,' she frowned. 'It's an organisation with integrity, a genuine desire to pioneer work in corrective cosmetics—they won some award a month ago——'

'Yes, I was rather pleased with that,' said Ruan implacably. 'It was from work I'd instigated. Dear me, I hope I'm not getting a good reputation!' he said sarcastically. 'That would be too difficult for you to accept, wouldn't it? Perhaps I should blacken myself a little. Are you still refusing to be nice to me, Natasha?'

'More than ever,' she said vehemently.

'Now wait a minute,' said David quickly. 'We—we can come to some arrangement. She's a little upset at your little... teasing. Of course we want to co-operate. Whatever you want, she'll do it——'

'No, she won't!' yelled Natasha. 'He wants me to sleep with him!'

'Is that all? Good grief, if that's his price, tell him you will!'

Her mouth opened in astonishment and she stared at David as if she could barely believe what he'd said, that he put his business interests above hers. He'd always taken care of her, soothed her fears when Ruan had been 'working' late, sympathising with her.

'*Give* myself to him?' she gasped.

'Why not? What's sex? Nothing! You don't have to enjoy it! When you consider what's at stake, the price of a night with him is hardly a sacrifice,' said David heatedly.

She couldn't believe her ears. All she could think of was that David had chanced everything on the Fondé contract and desperation was making him irrational.

'I'm sorry, David,' she said tightly. 'But it's out of the question! You must realise that.'

'You can't be so selfish!' shouted David.

'My body——' she began proudly.

'—is a temple,' explained Ruan with mock solemnity. 'That, David, means that she's never the one to make the sacrifices—other people do. And you will suffer because of her stubbornness.'

'Natasha, you've got to do this!' said David hoarsely.

'I can't, I won't! Can't you see what he's doing to us? What's happened to you?' she cried, the tears starting in her eyes. 'You're my protector! You comforted me when Ruan left; you sat with me for hours, holding me, cuddling me——'

'Kissing you?' suggested Ruan languidly.

She looked at him quickly. There was nothing mocking in his face, only a strange stillness as if he was trying to tell her something. And she couldn't answer, because yes, David had kissed her. She frowned. It had been like a brother's kiss. Hadn't it?

'I——' She bit her lip, her eyes enormous with doubt.

'Another lesson, Natasha,' said Ruan softly. 'No one does anything for someone else. They do it for themselves. If David kissed you, it was because *he* wanted to. Not because he thought you needed tenderness.' His face was impassive when she let out a small sob but his voice shook slightly. 'Shall we begin the interview?'

'Oh, God!' groaned David in hoarse despair. 'Natasha, do something!'

'I think he wants you to strip for me,' Ruan said mockingly. But she was frozen with shock.

David slumped into a chair, his face a sickly green. 'God, I can't believe my bad luck! You, the owner! How?' he croaked. 'You've never had the kind of money——'

'Oh, come!' scolded Ruan. 'You of all people must know that one doesn't need money of one's own to acquire things.' Natasha frowned at David's goggle-eyes. She could almost smell his fear. Her body tensed. There was more to come. 'So often,' continued Ruan with a sigh, 'people are fooled by my casual manner into underestimating me.' His tone became sinister. 'It's a fatal mistake. It may distress you to know that I've been very successful.'

'But how, I wonder?' asked Natasha grimly, gradually steeling herself to the unknown blows Ruan meant to land on her head. 'If you've made a mint of money it's probably from peddling drugs and you're using the beauty company as a front!'

'Of course,' he said sarcastically. 'I'm not smart enough to have made my fortune legally, am I, Natasha?'

She sensed a rippling anger behind his implacable mask. But she was too upset to care, the awful implications whirling around her head. She raised her pale face to Ruan's and was instantly impaled by the cruelty in his piercing eyes.

'So you've come to gloat,' she said shakily. 'To exult over the expressions on our faces as we come to terms with losing everything we've ever wanted.'

'I've come to interview you,' he corrected smoothly. 'And to make you a proposition. Where shall we go?'

'I won't be propositioned by you, so is there any point in carrying out this charade?' she snapped.

His mouth curved into an unpleasant smile. 'I told you before, you can persuade me if you wish.'

'Oh, dear God!' she whispered, every bone in her body weakening at the kind of persuasion he was expecting.

'Do it!' urged David vehemently. 'Anything! Let him have whatever he wants! Take her into the drawing-room, Ruan, and make her see sense. You have my permission to——'

'No, no, *no*!' she raged in despair.

'David,' said Ruan drily, 'I don't want you around. You cramp my style. Disappear for a few hours and take Caroline with you, will you?'

'Yes, yes. Sure.'

Rooted to the spot, Natasha watched wide-eyed as he hurried out, all too eager to please. And she began to quiver uncontrollably, Ruan's earlier threat pounding in her head. He'd sworn to get her, one way or another. And now the moment had come.

The room began to spin, faster and faster till she was too giddy to stand. With a low, guttural cry, she flung out her arms and felt herself rising into the air. She wanted to scream because she knew Ruan would take advantage of her frailty, but she seemed to be paralysed.

She felt his arms tighten around her, movement as if he was walking swiftly with her, a softness against her back. A mattress? She struggled to move her heavy limbs, to clear the whirling mist that veiled her eyes, and saw Ruan's face, dark, menacing, coming closer and closer...

Her mind went blank. And there was nothing but a frightening black void, swallowing her up.

CHAPTER SIX

SOMETHING soft pressed into her face, like a cloth, dabbing...warm. Warm...? Long, delicate fingers were stroking her brow. Then her lips. Or was it a mouth?

Hazily, Natasha tried to bring herself back to the present, though she wanted the gentle touching to continue because it was soothing and she needed to be calmed. But not, she thought with a sudden realisation, by Ruan!

She snapped her eyes open in alarm to find herself horizontal, obviously in grave physical danger, with Ruan's face inches away, his eyes dark and melting, his mouth... She gulped, wanting to be kissed, her lips pouting softly in unknowing demand.

'Are you tempting me or am I tempting you?' murmured Ruan huskily.

'Please!' she croaked in a threadbare whisper.

'I wondered when you'd ask,' he mocked.

His mouth claimed hers in a flurry of kisses that made her head spin again. She lay helpless, every inch of her focused on their lips, the incredible sweetness that sought to quench her hunger and yet only succeeded in arousing it more. She couldn't get enough of his kisses and was astonished when her hands slid to link around the nape of his neck, driving his lips more insistently against hers.

'Why...?' She gave up wondering why, the moment his tongue teased along the highly curved bow. Warm sensation flooded through her like a fast-running spring tide flashing up the Percuil river, obliterating all before it.

'Why not?' he whispered into her mouth.

His breath husked into the sensitive moistness and she savoured its fluttering exploration, wanting to feel the slide of harshly expelled air slip past her teeth and fill her mouth again with welcome warmth.

'Hate you,' she muttered reluctantly, her heart pounding so violently that it was making the blood in her ears roar.

'I know. I know. It makes no difference, though.'

This time she inhaled as he spoke and quivered from the sensation as her lips and tongue shimmered and tingled with pleasure.

'Ruan...' she whispered faintly, knowing he was drowning her, holding her head under water, taking her to the depths...

'Shhh.' His finger pressed against her protesting, passion-swollen mouth.

Natasha nuzzled it. She hadn't meant to but she couldn't help it; caution and wisdom had deserted her, leaving only a raw, wanton abandon and a desire to please her senses for once. His finger lightly drifted over her lips and to the deep velvety groove above them. She quivered when the small hairs lifted to his delicate touch, her enormous eyes half drowsy beneath the fluttering lashes. His fingers skimmed beneath the creamy soft skin of her chin, lingering on the flawless smoothness of her throat. Which he kissed.

Natasha moaned as her body arched. 'Ruan——'

His mouth was warming her collar-bone, slowly dropping small kisses along one side and then the other. She shut her eyes in ecstasy, shutting her mind to who he was, what he was. But then she felt his body shift, heard his male grunt of appreciation, and realised her breasts were in his hands, being stroked, kissed, suckled...

She bucked beneath him, unwittingly thrusting her breasts more surely towards his eager, hungry mouth. Appalled, she could only croak hoarsely and he seemed to take that as uncontrollable need because he shuddered and drew more deeply on the hard, quivering nipple that was sending such electric shocks into her system that she couldn't think clearly.

Softly his mouth encircled one rosy peak, one hand pacifying the other firm bud, which seemed eager to be caressed. There was a look on Ruan's face of such agonised bliss that it made Natasha's erratically leaping heart miss a beat or two. His face was dark against the white of her body, his lashes long and thick, closed over the terrible, cynical eyes on glorious lushness as his lips tasted her sweet body with a famished eagerness that tore every one of her nerves to shreds.

'Tasha,' he said, in a long whispering sigh, nibbling gently as his mouth moved from one breast to the swell of its twin.

She placed her hands on his head, wonderingly touching his hair, threading her fingers through it, and then her hands clenched into desperate fists when she felt him undoing her skirt.

'No,' she moaned, barely audible.

'Oh, yes,' he growled, his ardour unquenchable. He wrenched at the button roughly and she realised he expected her total surrender—and that she'd stupidly led him to believe that was what she had in mind too.

His mouth enclosed hers painfully and she struggled ineffectually against his weight, his determined fingers, his ruthless kiss and her own need. She had appetites, she thought in dismay. Appetites only a man like Ruan could satisfy. Waves of eroticism drove all thought from her head as Ruan whispered against her mouth, flattering her, crooning to her in Italian.

He seemed hardly to know what he was doing, the words of love and desire flowing over her like the warm, rippling summer sea. And she realised that it was an undeniable aphrodisiac to know that a man as insular and as strong-minded as Ruan should be losing control because of his need for her.

Her body writhed beneath his, no longer struggling but answering its own demands in defiance of her brain— willing him to make love to her. 'Oh, Ruan,' she husked jerkily into his ear. She nibbled the lobe and he quivered. The power that she felt, to reduce him to desire her— *her* made her feel light-headed.

Her mouth savoured the smooth line of his jaw and all the while small moans of pleasure were sounding in her throat. She wanted to look at him, to see his face, and slowly she lifted her lashes, her gaze sensual in its innocent allure.

His eyes flickered and glinted. 'Slut,' he whispered. 'Or, more accurately, *whore*!' His teeth clenched as if he was in pain and then his body had left hers and her hands were lying limply on her ravaged body.

'What——?'

'Surprised?' he drawled.

'W-w-what?' she stuttered huskily.

'I'm far too experienced in the ways of women to be fooled by you,' he said coldly. 'I've had years of practice in sublimating my needs. I can turn off whenever I want. It was interesting to watch your attempt, but you'll never get through to me with simulated sex. No woman will. Ever.'

She swallowed hard and took one appalled look at him then drew her blouse over her throbbing breasts in agonised shame, seeing the blush creep over their curves before she hid them from his sight and hers.

'Oh, my God, you bastard!' she whispered, trying to do up the buttons.

He pushed her fumbling, useless hands away, crouching beside the sofa. Sofa, she thought nervously, only now aware of that fact. At least he hadn't dragged her up to a bedroom. His fingers were firm and decisive, deftly flicking each button into place, and it galled her that he should be so calm when she was in a turmoil. If her own hands would stop trembling, she'd take over.

'There,' he said softly. Their eyes met. Slate-blue, stone-black. She shut hers tightly but he shook her, his hands crushing her shoulders as he did so. 'No,' he grated. 'Look at me!' He pulled her chin up and she was forced to do so, knowing he could see the abject misery she felt. 'I'm amazed you have such nerve,' he muttered. 'David tells you to behave like a whore pleasing a client and you give it a whirl!'

Her mouth dropped open in utter indignation. 'No!' she cried vehemently. 'I fainted—and before I could come round your hands were all over me——'

'Of course,' he said in a false, soothing voice. 'I made all the running and you did your best to stop me from the moment you realised what I was doing.' He gave a sarcastic laugh.

She trembled as sharp longing penetrated her loins and when she spoke her voice had become croaky. 'You confused me,' she said lamely, distraught that he could imagine she'd stoop to seducing him.

'You mean . . . I've mistaken the situation?' he asked unemotionally.

'*Yes!*' she cried eagerly, scrambling up to a sitting position and trying to tuck in her blouse.

'Allow me.'

His hands had swooped to her waist, pushing the silky material into her skirt, his long fingers expert and knowing. And she fixed her eyes hard on his tie-pin so that she could ignore the press of each fingerpad on the rising flesh of her buttocks, her sensitive spine, and, after he'd put his hands under her armpits to bring her to her feet and gently turn her around, the firm pressure of his aroused body against her back and the wonderful massage of his palms on her flat stomach.

Angrily she pulled away, staggered and grabbed the marble mantelpiece, panting slightly and bewildered. 'I don't know how it happened,' she said unhappily, her eyes as haunted as a hunted doe's. 'I don't know how I could have...' Her head shook slowly in dismay. 'Only that I didn't want it, any of it. I swear, on my life, I swear!' she cried, almost hysterical.

He stood with his legs straddled, hands thrust into his trouser pockets, every inch a supercilious, victorious male. 'And I—perhaps anyone watching—would have thought you were more than eager! Amazing how misunderstandings can occur, isn't it?' he observed in a deadly tone.

Natasha blinked. Slowly she scanned his implacable face. 'If that was another lesson, you're repeating yourself,' she rasped harshly, unable to credit that he could be so cruel and so utterly cold-blooded. Surely he couldn't have pretended to seduce her merely to force her into wondering if she'd been mistaken about his criminal activities?

'Sometimes,' he murmured, 'the message needs to be driven home to slow-witted children who don't listen the first few times.' He flashed her an insincere smile. 'Do you think there's a housekeeper in this mausoleum?'

'A what?' she said faintly, incapable of keeping up with his swift mind.

'I need a coffee. However, I'm sure you'd like something to calm your nerves.' He strode towards her and she shrank back against the wall but he only reached above her head and tugged at a fringed damask bell-pull, ignoring the closeness of their bodies as if she were a piece of furniture. 'There's a drinks tray on the sofa-table,' he said in a conversational tone. 'Would you prefer something stronger?'

'Coffee,' she muttered, making her way to a Georgian chair and crossing her shaking legs protectively. Ruan's assessing gaze toured their entire length from ankle to thigh. 'What are you going to do now?' she asked in a low voice.

He kept her waiting for his answer, smiling at the quickening of her breath as his glance sardonically toured the length of her body. 'Interview you—in a more conventional way,' he drawled eventually. 'Vertically.'

'Why?' she mumbled miserably, through parched lips. 'Interview me, I mean,' she added, to spike the amused reply he obviously had on the tip of his tongue.

'Because Fondé are far too particular for just anyone to take up their franchises,' he explained, moving to stand like an arrogant lord in front of the beautifully carved fireplace. 'Ah, the housekeeper,' he said, when a knock sounded discreetly on the door. 'Enter!'

'Good morning, sir,' said the woman respectfully.

'Morning. We're guests of Mr Veane,' smiled Ruan, charming the housekeeper effortlessly. 'This is Natasha Trelawny——'

The confused Natasha could see the housekeeper melting beneath Ruan's deceptively friendly expression. He'd always got on well with older women, she mused. Winifred, for instance. She realised the housekeeper and Ruan were looking at her expectantly.

'How do you do?' she said quietly, shaking the woman's hand. 'I'm——' She hesitated, looking at Ruan uncertainly, then decided to defy his threat. 'I'm going to take on the position of head beautician.'

'Welcome! It's an exciting idea, isn't it? I'm Mrs Dawkins.'

'Ruan Gardini, Fondé of Paris.' He clasped the woman's hands warmly in his, the grin dazzling and apparently sincere. 'We're all thrilled. I do hope nothing spoils the venture. It is such a worthwhile project.'

'Oh, yes, sir,' beamed Mrs Dawkins, evidently smitten. 'My Doreen's got a nasty birthmark on her front. Stops her sunbathing.'

'I hope the clinic can do something for your Doreen,' said Ruan, sounding concerned. 'Book her in, Miss Trelawny, and send the bill to me.'

'Oh, Mr Gardini!' beamed Mrs Dawkins. 'That's a handsome offer! I can see I'll have to look after you nice. What can I get you, sir?'

'Coffee, please, Mrs Dawkins,' purred Ruan. 'And a few biscuits for a desperately hungry man?'

'Leave it to me, sir,' said the housekeeper firmly, giving him a conspiratorial wink. 'I got two strapping sons of my own. I know what you men are like.'

'Splendid,' grinned Ruan. 'I seem to need refuelling frequently,' he admitted.

'Mr David likes his food, too,' confided Mrs Dawkins. 'Never stops eating. Let's see ... I've got a nice box of chocolate biscuits and a freshly baked Dundee—or would you like Death By Chocolate?'

'I can't think of a better way to go,' laughed Ruan.

'I'll bring them all,' said the housekeeper happily, hurrying off to prepare the coffee.

Ruan stretched luxuriously. 'Oh, the pleasure of it all!'

'You must be enjoying every moment of this,' Natasha said sullenly.

'It's been a delight from the moment I turned the balloon's basket over so that I could land on top of you,' he said, his mouth twitching with amusement. 'Now, Miss Trelawny,' he continued without a break, 'what makes you think you are worthy of my franchise?'

'I won't be part of your stupid teasing,' she snapped.

'This is no tease. Convince me that you're good enough and I'll make sure that everything you need for the salon is flown out on the next plane,' said Ruan surprisingly. 'I swear. On my mother's head.'

She tried to find some get-out clause in what he'd said but his promise seemed watertight. 'Why?'

'Very ungracious,' he commented. 'I think it's commercially sound and it fits in with my plans.'

With nothing to lose, she stiffly told him of her qualifications while they drank rich Arabic coffee and munched their way through a mountain of Mrs

Dawkins's chocolate biscuits, slender slices of the dark, rich cake and the moist Dundee, and Ruan questioned her closely as if he really was interested.

She began to get into her stride, detailing the work she'd done and the courses she'd attended. 'I spent my leisure time at the London salon,' she said earnestly, 'watching the two girls from Hong Kong and picking up tips from them on the art of massage. So I never stopped perfecting my technique, really.'

'Must have ruined your social life,' he observed. 'What did you do with the rest of your leisure time?'

'Slept,' she said ruefully. She caught his querying eyebrow and remembered she'd suggested that her life had been one long social whirl. But she was tired of deception. 'I put all my energies into work,' she told him quietly.

'What were your impressions of London?' he asked. 'I need to know, because you might find it too quiet by comparison down here and leave after a month or so. I want stability in the senior management staff.'

'I hated it,' she said frankly. 'I know it's a beautiful city, historic, buzzing with life, and I imagine it suits someone like you very well. But I was homesick all the time—for the kind of life I love: space to breathe, friendly people who have time for you—all the little things that make the pace of life gentler and kinder. Like supermarket check-out girls actually helping you with your shopping, and talking to you.'

'If you were homesick, why didn't you come back?' he murmured.

Because of you, she thought. You'd left your mark on every inch of this place. 'London offered me a chance to achieve my ambitions,' she said. 'If I'd stayed here or remained a hairdresser in London instead of studying hard, I might never have reached this important point in my life——'

'Which is?' he asked silkily, his eyes unfathomable.

'Fondé's products—your products,' she amended carefully, hoping to flatter his ego, 'are the best in the world and I want to work with them.' She leaned forward, intent on persuasion, her face impassioned. 'Ruan, whatever you think of David's behaviour or mine, you'll be the first to admit that people can jump to conclusions. You've tried to ram that point home to me often enough. So admit you might be wrong about us.'

'What I've seen and heard, what I know,' he said grimly, 'has only confirmed my beliefs.'

'I'm talking about four years ago,' she said earnestly. 'I didn't deliberately engineer the downfall of your sub-aqua business and neither did he. And he honestly was comforting me when you barged in.'

'You didn't see his eyes,' growled Ruan.

'Oh, Ruan, I don't know if he was kissing me from self-interest or not, only that I thought he was, but what does it matter?' she asked in exasperation.

'It matters,' he said softly.

'You and your Sicilian pride!' she said crossly. 'Look at this from a business point of view. The health clinic scheme is a good one and worthy of your franchise.'

'Go on. Coax me more,' he challenged.

Win or lose, she'd never forgive herself if she didn't try. Maybe he'd laugh and turn her down when she'd finished, but at least she'd know for the rest of her life that she'd put her trust in a spiteful, vengeful man.

She took a deep breath. Everything hung on her attitude and what she said. So she let herself go, all her passion for her work ringing in her warm, husky voice. 'This will be the first Fondé outlet in Britain. With a huge advertising campaign emphasising the natural products and their origins, we'll invite an enormous amount of media interest,' she enthused, knowing how important that was. 'I can see shots of the jungle, the researchers talking to local hunters, people working in the labs, and—oh, Ruan, how about a shot of the products being unloaded on Penmellin beach?'

'In barrels?' By men in striped jerseys, black eye-patches, sea-boots and cutlasses?' he suggested sardonically.

'All right,' she said grudgingly. 'I'll leave the PR to you. I'm one of the best beauticians you can get——'

'But I could train and set up beauticians to handle our products in major stores. What do I need with Tredinnick and you?' he murmured.

'It's different! In the stores, you'd be competing with all the other products. It would make you just like everyone else!' she cried eagerly. 'Whereas this way, you come in as a company offering corrective therapy treat-ments, which is much more appealing to your image, isn't it? And it's the luxury end of the market. Women would pay especially to come to Tredinnick. It's a won-derful retreat from the polluted air of city life and the noise. It's perfect for stress reduction, with walks through the garden, the river, the wonderful views——'

'True.'

She saw a softening of his eyes, their shade a gentle velvet-green now, and she drove her argument further, almost on the edge of her chair with eagerness, her eyes bright and sparkling like the pure water in the spring.

'You can't deny that having your company products associated with simple, peaceful surroundings and our slow Cornish ways is appealing,' she said huskily.

'Back to nature,' he said thoughtfully. 'Sparkling clear springs, unpolluted air and water, gentler lifestyle... Mmm. I'm getting the picture.'

'Add to that the fact that I'd have a team of people devoting themselves to teaching clients how to minimise disfigurement, and you have a really worthwhile cause,' she argued.

'The PR department will love it,' he conceded.

'Of course they will!' she said confidently. 'Clients will walk out of those gates fitter, more relaxed and more self-assured than when they came in. And that's money in the bank for you and job satisfaction for us.'

Ruan put the delicate bone-china cup on the wine table beside him and leaned back in his chair. 'Tell me about your techniques for reducing stress.'

She smiled, feeling hopeful. He couldn't be such a heel that he'd prevent her from helping people to look their best. 'Let's start with massage. As I said, the one I've evolved is a combination of Western and Oriental and is very thorough. Using your aromatic oils, I can ease headaches, relax tensions, relieve worries for a while. I can make lonely, unloved people feel a sense of their own worth and give them the satisfaction of being beautifully pampered. Being a beautician isn't catering for the vain, Ruan,' she said, deadly serious about the benefits of her work as always. 'If a woman—especially one with skin problems—looks as good as she can and someone has spent time considering her every need, she feels wonderful. A different person. It's lovely, being cherished.'

'Is it?' he muttered.

Startled out of her happy reverie, she looked at him intently and saw that he appeared to be brooding about something. And a sudden intuition told her that since his mother had died no one had cherished him. Women might throw themselves at him, come running whenever he clicked his fingers, but that wasn't the same. A deep desire to hold him in her arms and rock him swept over her.

'A massage would probably work wonders for you too,' she said, and then wished she hadn't spoken without thinking.

'It's on the agenda,' he said softly. 'Just as soon as the products arrive.'

'Oh! I didn't mean...' She frowned. '*What* did you say?' Her face cleared and a glimmer of hope began to filter into her mind but she didn't dare get too excited. 'You're taking me on?'

'Oh, yes. I'm taking you on. I said you could persuade me.'

She looked at him doubtfully. 'I don't understand why you're giving me exactly what I want,' she said slowly. 'Unless it's for the sheer pleasure it will give you to take it away again.'

'Once the contract is signed,' he said, 'you'll have no worries. Except...'

His softly sinister words hung in the air and her hopes fell. 'Except what?'

'I would break the contract if you gave me good reason.'

Natasha shuddered. He'd find a reason. 'I see. You said I'd have to stew, to suffer. And what better than slow torture?' she said bitterly. 'You mean to keep me on tenterhooks, spending my time wondering how soon it will be before you smash my dreams, with the Sword of Damocles over my head! Will you wait till the business is up and running before you create mayhem?'

His eyes glittered briefly and then became expressionless. 'It would be better than ending it now,' he acknowledged. 'You see, there are ways of taking revenge, Natasha. You can hit out immediately and satisfy your initial temper. Or you can wait till the time is ripe—when an assault will cause the most pain.' A slow, sinister smile lifted the corners of his mouth. But not his cold, blank eyes. 'Only a fool hits a man who's down. It's better to wait till he's standing because he has further to fall and it hurts him more.'

'Oh, my God!' she whispered, appalled at his ruthlessness.

'You have the choice, Natasha. To walk away in case you're hurt and leave David to face the cost, or to stay and take the risk.'

'Do you want my answer now?' she asked tremulously, thinking that she must talk to David first.

'No. I want you to think your situation over and be absolutely sure that you've made the choice. Some time,' he said huskily, 'I must try your massage.'

'I only treat women,' she said, her throat dry. An image of Ruan, his honey-gold body beneath her fingers, was too unnerving to contemplate.

'There will be this one exception.' His voice had slid slowly over every word, as if he was contemplating her touch.

She gulped. She could get an assistant to be there too. Or the assistant could do the massage. 'There's no reason why I should——'

'Correct. Only that I rather relish the idea of you working on my body, like a Roman slave girl. It will help to make it clear to you what our relative positions are.'

'I see. You want to rub it in that——' She smiled wryly. 'OK. I rub it in,' she amended. Definitely she'd need a chaperon. 'After you've signed the contract,' she said curtly.

'Done. And now we can go out for lunch,' he said, the picture of contentment.

'No, thanks. I wanted to explore,' she demurred, 'to see where I'm to work, what David's done——'

'We'll have plenty of time for that. You'll come out with me,' he said, in a voice of absolute authority.

Ruan was making it clear what their positions were. He was in power. She was obligated to him. Natasha bit back her protest and dutifully followed him to his car. If she played docile, he'd relax his guard. And maybe she'd discover his next move before he made it and be able to take avoiding action.

They drove to St Mawes where he insisted on having his lunch served outside on the terrace of the Idle Rocks Hotel. They sat a few feet above the dark rocks which were being pounded by the waves. She lifted her face to the mist of spray and felt the fresh taste of salt on her lips. Seabirds scavenged in the seaweed-draped rock pools below and beyond, across the harbour, yachts lay at anchor by Place Manor.

Natasha's eyes were on the stern trawler, small, squat and heavy, moored to the small stone jetty which protected the small fishing community from the worst of the weather which came roaring up the Carrick Roads from the Atlantic Ocean. There came the sound of men mending a winch, the clang of metal, the rasp of a running chain, and she felt a lump well up in her throat.

'Thinking of your father?' asked Ruan quietly.

His hand lay over hers, comforting and undemanding. She nodded. 'It's a terrible, harsh life, fishing,' she mused. 'Why do people do it?'

He shrugged. 'Pride, heritage, love of the sea ...'

'But it's not like it was,' she argued. 'There aren't the huge shoals of pilchards and mackerel any more. The fishermen have to go further and further for their catches—take greater risks.'

'But they also have a deep satisfaction,' Ruan said quietly. 'They're in touch with the sea they love and the elements. Man against nature——'

'Storms,' she said, white-lipped.

'Ever crossed a road?' he asked mildly.

She took the point. 'OK. So life itself is dangerous.'

'Your father was happy,' Ruan told her. 'One of the happiest men I knew. He had a loving wife and a daughter he idolised. He'd had more joy in his life than many men experience. There was an enormous cameraderie among the fishing crews,' he added. 'Though you were too young to remember, I suppose.'

She felt a little better about her father's death. It had always seemed such a waste before. 'I remember Father and all the men swinging us, their children, into the air when we ran down to greet the boats,' she said slowly. Her face softened with tenderness. 'I remember the fishermen's choir, singing sea-shanties——'

'—on the quayside,' Ruan broke in, his voice very soft. 'We sat with our legs dangling over the edge and your wellington boot fell off into the water.'

She laughed, because she'd gone home in transports of delight. Ruan had solemnly insisted that she wore his boot, four sizes too large, while he'd walked beside her, quite indifferent to the holes appearing in his sock.

Oddly, Ruan's words had made her pain less bitter. Her father had been happy and she was glad. 'I'm beginning to understand the appeal of a fisherman's life,' she admitted. 'I still wish Father had worked in a bank,' she sighed. 'I expect Mother would have preferred that, too.'

'She loved the kind of man he was,' corrected Ruan. 'Strong, brave, a man who was comfortable with his life. Do you remember when I went to talk to her, after she'd forbidden you to see me?'

Natasha nodded. 'I remember,' she said softly. 'What did she say to you?'

She'd been madly in love with Ruan. Her loyalty to her mother had clashed with her strong feelings for the dare-devil 'bad boy' of Roseland.

'She told me that she didn't want you getting involved with me—not because I took risks, but because I was a loner,' he answered. 'Your father had the comradeship of working in a team. I had my own private, highly personal competition going on and she could see that I would roam the world, leaving you behind.'

'And that you'd have a girl in every port,' she said lightly, hiding her resentment.

'No,' he said quietly. His eyes lifted to hers and they were filled with such intensity that she felt that he'd pinned her to her seat. 'That's not true. She worried because she knew I was obsessive. And she feared that intensity—and what it might do to you.'

'She told *me* you were dating other girls under my nose,' muttered Natasha.

'And you believed her, as a loyal daughter should,' he said without rancour. 'She deceived you because she loved you. It was important in her eyes, you see, to save you from a greater hurt. But you persisted in seeing me, stubborn as ever. I couldn't help but find our continual intimacy highly arousing.' He smiled to himself. 'It's just as well David tagged along and became your chaperon. If we'd been alone more, I'm not sure I could have resisted the appeal you had for me then.'

'Are you pretending that you deliberately played it cool after your talk with my mother? I can't believe that you wanted to save me from being the little woman, waiting anxiously at home for her adventurous lover!' she scorned.

His mouth twisted wryly. 'It does sound a little too noble for me, doesn't it? After all, that would be the action of an unselfish and caring man,' he murmured, not answering her question. 'And we both know I'm none of those. It's incredible that I'd put your needs, your life, your future ahead of mine.' His hands reached up to undo her piled-up hair, and he stopped her protest with a gentle reproach. 'Let me.' His fingers threaded through her hair, spreading it on her shoulders, and she shook it free. 'There is no other woman like you,' he said softly, turning her hand over. He brought her palm to his lips and kissed along its lines, the tender gesture wrenching at her heart.

'Don't play the courtship game with me,' she said unhappily. 'I'm not fooled. I know what you're after.'

'I wonder.'

He leant back in the chair and called for the bill, his expression secretive. Natasha shielded her eyes against the dazzle on the sea and wondered why he was gazing so wistfully on the tiny cluster of fishermen's houses.

'You'd like to live here again, wouldn't you?' she said in a sudden flash of inspiration.

'To spend my time water-skiing, sailing, swimming, climbing up to Drake's Down in the teeth of a tearing gale...' He laughed dismissively. 'Don't you think I'd be bored in two weeks?' he said, flattening her pride in solving the reason for his inner yearning. 'This place sleeps after the pubs close. I'd be as mazed as a curley to stay long.'

She laughed with him at the old Cornish phrase which mocked the curlew's crazy flight and shrill piping. But she felt relieved. If she could bear to stick it out, he'd be gone soon, tired of playing the heavy gangster role, moving on to pastures new.

That afternoon, mindful of Natasha's high heels and slim skirt, they drove slowly around all their old haunts, both silent from the memories crowding in. Ruan sat motionless in the car and stared at the ruins of his cob home.

'Mother kept that with such pride,' he mused. 'She'd whitewash those walls every spring.'

Natasha sadly noted the verdigris, knowing how Bella Gardini would have been shocked at the state of the cottage. 'Most of the thatch has blown away,' she remarked. 'I can hear the wind whistling through the doors and windows.' Her eyes were misty. For all his faults, Ruan had found it in his heart to love his mother and to appreciate her unremitting hard work. 'It must be tough, seeing your home like this,' she said sympathetically.

'I can see her now,' he said in an infinitely soft growl. 'Bent over that damn step, scrubbing as if she meant to take an inch off it.'

A smile appeared shakily on Natasha's mouth. 'Dear Bella,' she said huskily. Slowly he turned to her, his own eyes molten black as though he longed to turn back the clock and to see his mother vigorously whitening the step again. 'Oh, Ruan!' Overcome, she held out her arms and he turned away, his shoulders high. Impulsively she placed her hands on his back and rubbed gently to soothe him.

'Don't,' he grated. 'I'm your enemy.'

'Only because you insist. We don't have to be enemies,' she said hopefully, continuing to touch him, believing that friends touched, enemies never did. 'Your mother liked to see us together. If she were alive,' she said hesitantly, 'would she be proud of what you're doing?'

He let out a long, shuddering breath. 'I think she'd understand,' he said after a pause.

'That's not what I asked.' His back was relaxing. She moved her fingers to the knots in his shoulders.

Ruan tipped his head back in pleasure. 'That's all the answer you're getting,' he muttered.

'Are you afraid of becoming friends with me again?' she asked gently.

He twisted around in the seat, his eyes wary. 'What the hell do you mean?' he demanded.

'I wondered if you felt bound to your idea of revenge,' she answered levelly. 'You felt you'd let your father down. You were obsessed with proving yourself. That's frightening.'

'Father always told me that the Gardinis avenged themselves tenfold,' he growled.

'Yes, but...' She wrinkled her brow. 'You're destroying yourself, Ruan, and I don't like to see that. You think you're destroying David and me, but your ruthless, calculating behaviour is also——'

'Do you think I don't know what I'm doing?' he asked softly. 'I know what's happening to me; I'm aware that I've become less than human, that an obsession has taken me over. That knowledge only intensifies my anger. I am perfectly aware of the kind of man I've become—and why I have to do what I'm doing. I have good cause, Natasha. Haven't I taught you not to judge without knowing all the facts?'

'You're suggesting I'm ignorant of them?' she said, puzzled. What more was there to know?

'I'm *telling* you that you are. And before you ask I would be a fool to confide in you. I still don't know for sure whether you're a greedy, selfish woman, or totally innocent.'

'I've *told* you,' she began indignantly.

'I know,' he said suavely. 'But the evidence is against you.'

She winced. 'Won't you ever trust anyone?' she asked sadly.

'I doubt it,' he said grimly. Then he sighed. 'I think we'd better go back. I want to see over Tredinnick before I sail.'

She was getting used to the sudden announcements of his plans. 'You're going? I thought——'

'I have some smugglers to meet at midnight,' he drawled. 'I'm a criminal, with illicit trysts, illegal deals, remember?'

Flushing, she subsided, her sympathy for him vanishing. She hated it when he kept throwing her words and opinions back at her. When they reached Tredinnick again and were met by the tense David, she felt like leaving them both and going to spend the evening with Mrs Dawkins. But she did enjoy seeing around the beautifully restored mansion, including the room which was to be hers, and quietly telling David that the franchise was probably theirs.

'Good girl,' said David approvingly, his eyes quickly assessing her appearance, as if wondering whether she and Ruan had used the casting couch. 'Well, that's it. You'll be going soon, then, Ruan?'

'I'm off tonight,' he answered, fingering the adjustable massage table with a little too much interest for Natasha's peace of mind. 'Do you have an office here?' he asked casually.

'Yes. But it's locked,' said David promptly.

'Then there's only the old attic left to see, where the servant's quarters used to be.'

'Oh, nothing up there,' said David casually. 'That's why I didn't bother taking you there.'

Ruan directed his laser stare at the awkwardly shifting David. 'Tash and I played look-out in the attic,' he murmured. 'You can see right down the creek to Smugglers' Cove. We pretended we were revenue men, watching for boats to draw up.' Natasha opened her mouth to say that his memory was playing him false; they'd pretended to be marooned in a lighthouse. But Ruan gripped her hand hard and gave her a quick, warning look which baffled her. 'I think I'll go up now and have a look, for sentiment's sake,' he said with a cheerful smile.

'Sentiment? You?' David sounded as astonished as she was. 'Don't waste your time, there's nothing up there,' he said quickly. 'Besides, the stairs are unsafe. That's why I've sealed them off.'

'Oh, you know me,' drawled Ruan, his green eyes gleaming. 'I thrive on risks.'

'This one's not worth taking,' said David flatly.

Natasha looked from one to the other, acutely aware that something was going on she didn't know about. Ruan suspected something; David was trying to stop him finding out. And it was something that was making David sweat with fear and shuffle his feet. But he'd always been straight—highly respected, an unimpeachable solicitor with a flawless reputation. So what skeleton was Ruan trying to haul out of David's cupboard?

'I never like to leave a stone unturned,' murmured Ruan. 'You never know what's lurking there, ready to crawl out.'

'Ruan,' said David a little shakily, 'I strongly advise you not to tackle those stairs. It would be highly dangerous. I know that's like a red rag to a bull as far as you're concerned, but I could virtually guarantee that you'd break your neck. You don't want Natasha to discover you dead in the morning, do you?' he finished with a rather unpleasant smile.

'I certainly don't,' agreed Ruan fervently, capitulating. 'So much for sentiment. I'd be wise to forget the fun we had as children. You're right. I'll leave you both to chatter about your plans and return tomorrow. I need a little excitement and I don't think Natasha's keen on supplying it.'

'Not tonight or any night,' she said coolly. 'Goodnight, Ruan. Come on, David, let's enjoy this time on our own.'

Deliberately she tucked her arm around his waist, excluding Ruan. But when he drove away she felt as if part of her was missing. She tried to enthuse over David's plans and to laugh at his jokes but it wasn't the same as being with Ruan. Although he was dangerous and made her stay on her guard most of the time, nevertheless she felt oddly at ease with him when he stopped persecuting her. It wasn't surprising; they'd been inseparable for all her formative years.

After supper, she and David sat in the candle-lit drawing-room and while he toasted his feet by the log fire and watched some rather mindless programmes on television she pulled back the heavy swagged curtains and curled up against a stack of huge cushions on the window-seat, staring out at the flickering light of a small fishing boat moored on the distant bend of the creek.

After a while, she stretched languidly. 'I think I'll turn in. Thank you for a lovely evening, David. I'm so happy to be here.'

He rose and came over, bending down to kiss her affectionately just as a car drew up outside, its lights sweeping across the window. Guiltily they both jumped apart and saw Ruan staggering out, his shirt undone at the throat, his tie twisted loose and a child's balloon in one hand.

'The man's drunk!' cried David in disgust.

'Ye-e-s,' said Natasha doubtfully. Ruan could always hold his liquor, and if anything he became quieter, more perfectly controlled, when he'd had a few pints. But this time he did look as if he was smashed out of his mind. 'I'm going upstairs,' she muttered grimly. 'I don't want to meet him in that state.'

She hurried out, shutting the drawing-room door firmly. When she was about halfway up the stairs, the front door opened. Looking back, she saw Ruan stumble in, intent on making his legs go where he wanted them to. He began to sing a bawdy Cornish rugby song and Natasha blushed with embarrassment, hurrying on, casting anxious, backward glances at his stumbling progress. Suddenly, he made for the stairs in a shambling rush, still apparently oblivious to her.

Ruan had hold of the dragon's tail at the top of the banister, and stopped his raucous song with a pleased cry. 'Hi, Tash! Are we goin' to have fun tonight!'

'You're drunk!' she said with disdain. 'Paralytic! Go and take a cold shower.'

She reached her new room with relief and listened with her ear pressed against the locked door. There was the shamble of dragging feet going towards the room at the far end of the landing that David had reluctantly allocated to Ruan. The door slammed and she breathed easy again.

Natasha settled down for the night, fully expecting to sleep easily because she was very tired. But there was too much running through her mind. In the early hours of the morning, she saw a dim light appear beneath her door as if someone was outside with a torch. She held her breath and after almost a minute it moved on, towards...

Wide awake, she sat up in bed, her heart thudding. The light had moved in the direction of the attic stairs.

There wasn't a sound. She flung off the bedclothes and ran to open her door a tiny bit. There was a small spot of light dancing up the corridor, occasionally blocked by Ruan's unmistakable bulk. She remembered the fishing boat in the creek. She remembered Ruan's mocking references to smuggling. Perhaps...

She closed the door softly and drew on her cotton-velvet robe over her nightdress. Barefoot, feeling her way along the walls, she padded along the corridor, her imagination seething with ideas.

Ruan was up to no good. If he wasn't signalling to the boat, perhaps, she thought melodramatically, he meant to set the house on fire. Perhaps his drunk act had been a pretence, to persuade them that he was harmless.

Harmless! she mouthed to herself in derision. As if he was ever.

The door to the attic which David had padlocked was now swinging open and the moon from the landing window behind her shone on the stairs dimly. She peered anxiously at them. To her surprise, they looked new. She frowned down at the treads, unable to equate this with what David had said.

'Odd, isn't it?'

The beam of a torch blinded her, but Ruan's mocking tones were unmistakable. Her eyes widened. His voice sounded clear and controlled and totally sober. 'You're not drunk,' she said accusingly.

'No, and these stairs aren't dangerous either,' he countered. 'Now why would David lie to me? Do you think he keeps his girlie magazines up here?'

'David doesn't have your base passions,' she snapped.

'No. He doesn't have passion at all. Only a cold love of money and the power it can bring him,' said Ruan harshly. 'He knows he can only buy respect, not earn it. As he's bought you.'

'That's not true!' she denied hotly.

'He has what you want. To take it, you have only to live here, to work here. Tempting, isn't it? What comes next, Natasha? Will he involve you in his fraudulent scheme until you're in it so deep you have to buy his silence with your body—or a ring on your left hand?' The torchlight danced over her face and she shut her eyes to its glare.

'Why don't you say exactly what you suspect?' she demanded tightly. 'What fraud?'

'Come up,' he said softly. 'I dare you.'

Fatally intrigued, Natasha ascended the stairs.

CHAPTER SEVEN

'BRAVO!' whispered Ruan in mock admiration when she reached the top. 'Wasn't it a dangerous climb? Now we've both risked our necks——'

'Don't be silly...' Her voice died away. The beam was exploring her robe, playing on the outline of her body, and she felt alarmingly vulnerable.

She was. Ruan pulled her to him and the warmth of him penetrated to her in a searing flash of heat. He didn't kiss her, despite the fact that her mouth had flowered, ready. Instead, he held her, smiling down on her, and she reluctantly compared the strength of his hand with David's limp, sweaty one.

His fingers brushed her breast and sensation flared out in tingling rays from her nipple, which had hardened in an instant.

'David didn't crawl into bed with you, then,' he husked. 'Was he too busy with Caroline, do you think?'

'She's gone away. What's this about a fraud? I know what you're trying to do,' she said coldly, ignoring the insolent liberty he was taking with her body, and his disgusting taunt. 'You want to put doubts in my mind about him. I'm not falling for all these hints of a dark secret,' she told him, lifting her head and pushing out a stubborn chin. 'If you start rumours that he's involved in something crooked——'

'It will finish him as a solicitor,' finished Ruan complacently.

Her eyes blazed with contempt. 'You'd go that far to avenge the few stolen kisses he took from the woman you thought was yours?'

'Solicitors are in a position of trust. If they act fraudulently, then they must be punished,' he said harshly.

'*If*,' she said coldly. 'The trouble is, you can't prove anything, can you?'

His eyes narrowed speculatively and he deliberately took her shoulders in a bruising grip. 'Defiant to the last,' he growled.

'I'm merely warning you,' she snapped. 'Persist in this slander and I'll act as witness for David to sue you for every penny you've got and demand that you substantiate your ludicrous claims.'

He smiled enigmatically. 'You're being loyal to the wrong man,' he said, and walked away from her.

She followed a short way and then stopped, nervous of the inky blackness. 'Ruan! Bring the light! I'm in the dark!' she complained.

'I know,' he called drily. 'It's your own fault.'

She fumed, unwilling to risk searching for the stairs. 'I don't like the dark, Ruan!' she called plaintively.

'I would have thought you'd got used to it, after all this time,' he said, unpityingly.

'Devil!' she muttered. She heard him wandering around the labyrinth of rooms over the bare floorboards, opening cupboards. 'What are you doing?' Her ears strained for tell-tale sounds. 'You—you haven't got any matches with you, have you?' The light bobbed towards her again and all she could see was a neon glow and Ruan's looming black figure, but his shoulders were hunched in menace and she cringed back a little, afraid.

'You honestly believe I'd torch Tredinnick?' he asked in a quiet growl.

She flushed. 'No, I suppose not. That would really bring an end to your dreams, wouldn't it?' He winced and she noticed for the first time the outline of a box under his arm. 'Found the skeleton in his cupboard?' she asked irritably, shivering in the cold.

'No, toys. Perhaps he's got an illegitimate child,' he said sarcastically.

'Don't be ridiculous!' she scorned. 'I'm freezing. Take me downstairs at once!'

'In a minute.' He put the box on a table and directed the light on it, lifting out a photograph album and flicking through the pages. She tried to see the pictures but he shut it with a snap.

'What is it?' she asked curiously. He ignored her, picking something else from the box, turning over in his hands a home-made model of St Mawes castle. His whole body had tensed as if he'd made a great discovery. 'Oh, stop it, Ruan!' she said irritably. 'I've had enough of your dramatics! Show me the way out!'

When he lifted his eyes to hers, she shuddered. They were lethal, promising unremitting revenge, and she'd never seen him look so angry and she'd never felt such fear. 'There's only one way out of this and I'll show you when I'm good and ready,' he rasped. 'And if I find you're mixed up in his evil scheme——'

She let out a furious exclamation and stormed off, stumbling into walls, trying to find the doorway. Her arm was caught and she was dragged to the top of the stairs, to the very edge, and terror clutched at her stomach because she knew he was very close to exploding with an uncontrollable rage and might do anything.

'Ruan, be sensible!' she scolded, feeling her old fear of heights weakening her resistance. He knew her vulnerability. Too often he'd held her hand on cliff paths, coaxed her, encouraged her along. That made it worse because he must know he was frightening her. 'Let go of my arm!' she demanded hoarsely. 'Shine the light so I can see where I'm going or I'll y-y-yell for David.'

'You're courageous,' he said grudgingly. 'I'll give you that.' He twisted her around, holding her close and peering at her face with blazing eyes. 'Courageous enough maybe to take risks that others would never dare. God, Natasha! You make me want to kill you sometimes!' he said savagely.

'Don't you ever let up?' she croaked.

'Never,' he growled. 'I keep on and on and on until I reach my goal. It's the way I've always worked. If you are part of David's unlawful scheming then take my advice: leave now while you're still in one piece. Because he won't be, by the time I've finished with him, and neither will anyone he's involved with.'

Her legs went watery and Ruan sensed this, tightening his hold on her, rocking on his feet so that they both swayed, taunting her with the long drop down the steep stairs.

'I'm not involved in any scheme,' she whispered, feeling hysterical. 'But you are. Why did you pretend to be drunk?'

'To make David think he could sleep in his bed without fear tonight,' he drawled.

'What are you planning?' she asked shakily.

His cruel mouth wiped out her fear of falling. His lips bruised hers with a violence that sought to brand her with his mark forever. His hands roamed insolently over her body, and, petrified, she didn't dare to move a muscle, but stood there quivering at the helplessness of her situation.

'Throw in your lot with me,' he urged. 'I'll have you as you are: flawed, conspiring . . . beautiful. I'll have you anyway, because I've set my mind on it. Talk to Caroline. She knows how single-minded I am. She's been with me for years. I will get what I want,' murmured Ruan into the soft skin behind her ear. His mouth nibbled the lobe and she gave a little moan. 'I want Tredinnick, you, and David's downfall. Help me and I'll make sure you get the beauty business for yourself, as your reward.'

Her mind was whirling, struggling to stay clear while the rhythm of his big hands set her body tingling. He

began to push up the fabric of her robe, drawing it up
slowly, to her shins, knees... 'Wait!' she husked.

His mouth drifted sweetly over hers. She wanted him.
But not as something to be lusted after. She loved
Tredinnick. But not at the price of her self-respect—and
she could never be disloyal to David when he'd done so
much for her. Desperately Natasha gritted her teeth
against Ruan's sensual assault, trying to think of a way
to free herself from his grasp.

'Tasha!' he crooned. 'You smell delicious. Look
gorgeous——' His voice became muffled. 'Feel ...
wonderful.'

She moaned and gripped his shoulders, her frantic
hands digging into the flesh beneath the thin shirt. His
fingers had worked up both robe and nightdress while
she'd been trying to focus her mind and... She gulped,
straining away. But he was boldly caressing the firm
muscles of her naked buttocks, making them contract
in an unnerving rhythm.

Her eyes opened wide in alarm. 'No, Ruan!' she
pleaded huskily. 'I can't think... and come... to a decision... while—ohhh!' she groaned as his hands swept
firmly up the sweet dipping curve of her back. 'I
want——'

She clenched her teeth. She'd almost begged him to
slide his hands downwards again, to continue the
mindless rhythm, because now she felt cheated, her whole
body pressing into his wantonly, demanding satisfaction.

'And I want you!' he muttered thickly, kissing her like
a man possessed. 'I want you and I'll do almost anything to have you. To hold you in my arms, naked,
willing, begging.' His eyes glittered down, mesmerising
her, and she felt her heart leap and thud violently against
his hard, crushing chest. 'I want to spend a night stroking
your skin,' he breathed, tense excitement pouring off his
straining body. 'I want to forget everything and luxuriate
in your body, the curves, the luscious swells...'

She felt as if she were floating. His fingers were moving in tandem with his words, sliding sensuously around the arc of each breast. Her head tipped back. Dreamily she touched the angle of his jaw with her palm and let it enjoy the smooth skin.

He began to undo her robe. Natasha dimly realised that she was on the brink—not only literally, but emotionally and physically—and she knew she had to do something to allow herself to draw back or she'd be committing herself to a man who was without a shred of decency——

But with a disconcerting ability to seduce her wanton body.

'Oh, Ruan, you can't ask me to betray David,' she managed, in a harsh croak.

'Mmm?' He let the robe slip to the floor and lightly tested the weight of each breast beneath the soft, caressing fabric of her nightgown. Natasha shuddered as violently as he did. 'God, I need you!' he breathed fiercely.

She wanted to back away, but someone had glued her feet to the floor. 'Not here!' she cried apprehensively.

'On the edge of a precipice?' he smiled gently, his head indicating the stairs. 'Exciting. Dangerous.' Arrogantly he pressed his hand to her stomach and began to slide it very, very slowly downwards over the material of her nightdress, not taking his eyes off her for a moment.

Her brain persuaded her reluctant hand to arrest the movement. 'Please stop!' she husked.

'Touch me,' he growled.

'I couldn't!' She licked her lips and saw his eyes kindle.

'Touch me,' he ordered softly. He took her hand and laid it on his chest, his eyes hot with desire. 'Touch me,' he whispered. 'Caress me.'

His satin voice glided into the core of her body. Wanting to, driven by something she couldn't control, she let her hand drift across his chest and then in a daze slowly undid each button so that he could shrug off the shirt. Her palms slid up the hot silk of his skin, marvelling at the power of his beautiful body.

She looked up at him and he was staring down at her with unfathomable eyes. A dread slowly filled her that he was merely going through the motions because he wanted revenge more passionately than he wanted her. She froze.

'David,' she said huskily. 'The fraud. What is it?' He didn't answer. He seemed incapable of moving for a moment, just staring at her, his eyes suddenly bleak. 'Ruan!' she said in panic. 'I have a right to know! Tell me about him!'

'My God!' he growled, his voice slightly slurred. 'You switch on and off like a neon sign in Piccadilly. I want *you* to tell me about him. Where he goes and what he does——'

'Spy on him?' she whispered.

'Yes.' As if in regret, he slowly pushed her away, then groaned and caught her face between his warm, welcoming hands, kissing her with a restrained passion that inexplicably touched her heart. 'I have to go,' he muttered.

'Go?' she repeated in a dazed way, yearning to stay there all night, kissing. Only kissing. His hand pushed distractedly through his hair and she saw that he was shaken. That affected her more than anything could have done. 'Oh, Ruan!' she said tremulously. 'I wish——'

'Don't say it!' he snarled. 'I can't deal with the sadness of wishes. They're waiting for me. I must go.'

She followed the abrupt jerk of his head. The boat was in the creek, flashing a light. Grimly Ruan waved the torch in answer. 'You're not...!' The words stuck in her throat.

'Don't worry,' he said sardonically. 'I won't get caught. The revenue men are busy in Falmouth, investigating a suspicious-looking yacht that sailed in this morning.'

Natasha frowned. 'How do you know?'

'You know how things spread around here. It's all round the town. I'm late. Find out what you can. I'll be back in a few days.' The flat of his hand moved over her body, moulding it firmly, only the tightness of his mouth and the brittle light in his eyes betraying the fact that he was slowly bringing himself under control. 'Take the torch,' he said. 'I need a moment or two up here alone.' She hesitated. 'Go!' he scowled. 'Or I'll choose pleasure before business.'

She scurried away. She had her release—and wished she'd been held a captive because then she could pretend that she had no choice but to suffer his lovemaking. Whereas now, free from his clutches, she felt only frustration and resentment.

In her room, she lay shivering beneath the bedclothes, listening, her mind and her body all but consumed by thoughts of him. He came along the corridor, sure-footed in the dark, hurried down the main stairs and out of the front door. She heard the crunch of his feet on the gravel and the car started up.

Her body slumped in desolation. If Ruan was obsessive, so was she. With him. He was corrupting her, slowly but surely. Perhaps that was his revenge: to turn the pure virgin into an abandoned whore. To make her run to him of her own volition. That moment was closer than he knew.

She shook uncontrollably, unsure of her strength to resist him again. At least if he was going on some illicit operation she'd have a few days of peace.

Peace maybe, but not rest. When Ruan returned a few days later, she was walking in the valley, hoping to tire herself out, trying to control the constant destructive need that raged in her empty body and the longing to see him again. Every car that had driven up the lane to the house had sent her into a state of agitation, her mouth drying, her hands trembling with anticipation.

Now she heard the hungry purr of a powerful engine and knew he'd come back at last. Suddenly illogically afraid, incapable of facing him, she ran to hide between two stone walls. She realised it must be the old cattle-rush that stopped animals from roving into the estate when the drovers brought them down to the river. Even here, she thought bitterly, Ruan had left a memory—of a warm summer afternoon when they'd hidden here from David so they could kiss one another in private.

'Tasha!'

She sighed in defeat. He was coming in her direction. 'Here,' she said listlessly.

He homed in on her like a plane on a beacon, his sharp sense of hearing immediately locating where she was. He leaned over the stone wall of the rush, smiling, his smoke-blue chamois jacket discarded and hooked around one finger, crisp white sleeves rolled up to show his muscular arms.

And he looked so delighted to see her and his face seemed so open and happy that an infinite, irrational sense of serenity stole over her.

'You look absolutely gorgeous,' he said softly, his eyes admiring. 'I've brought you something.' He held out a spray of pink camellia blossoms, their soft petals gleaming among the glossy green foliage.

'Oh, Ruan!' she breathed brokenly. He leaned forward and tucked it in her hair as he had when they'd first discovered the bush which was blooming with pre-cocious eagerness in the centre of the overgrown maze. Her eyes shone.

'So. What have you been doing?' he asked lightly, his eyes veiled.

'Oh, sorting the beauty-rooms, stacking the Fondé boxes that came yesterday,' she said with a sigh. That should have excited her, but it hadn't. He was even taking that pleasure from her. 'Nothing much.'

'And the evenings?'

She noticed the sinews of his arms contracting and saw he'd clenched his fists as he waited for her answer. He really did hate the thought of David being in the same house, she thought.

'David watched television. I got bored,' she admitted.

'I'm not surprised,' he said drily. 'What else has he been doing?'

'Going to the office.' It had worried her that the details of David's day had bored her.

'Did he mention the bank?'

She frowned, wondering if they'd made some financial arrangement. 'Yes, he went there, and to the post office to send some letters, Pengelly's for some socks and the travel agent for a few holiday brochures,' she said, with faint sarcasm. 'I could tell you about the clients he saw and what they said, if you want.'

Ruan smiled. 'Likes chatting to you, doesn't he?' he observed. He took her hand. 'Life with David must be tedious. I'm glad to be back.'

'Was... was your mission successful?' she mumbled.

'Tash!' he said with affection, kissing the top of her head. 'I was kidding you along. I met a few old friends. We had a sail, a few beers, sang a few songs. We pitted our wits against the sea and nothing more. I swear. I'm glad to get on shore and stretch my legs, though. I feel I've been confined for too long.' He smiled warmly. 'It's a wonderful morning. Like to come for a run?' he suggested.

Natasha hesitated, but she'd been bored out of her mind and had taken little physical exercise in the last few days, other than her daily routine. Suddenly the discovery that Ruan had done nothing worse than carouse with a few friends made her feel like unleashing her energy.

'A run would be nice,' she said cautiously. 'Down the valley and along the beach?'

'Then inland up to Windmill Hill,' he suggested, helping her over the stile.

'I'll be dead beat, going that far,' she groaned, and left her hand in his as they walked together towards the upper garden. His hand was firm and capable. It had held her safe when he'd taught her to swim and he'd conquered her fear of water, and the time when they'd scrambled into the caves to explore in the dank darkness and only his presence had stopped her from running away. While she was with Ruan, it had seemed that no harm could ever come to her.

'But I need the exercise,' said Ruan, coaxing her expertly. 'I need someone who's fit enough to keep up with me. I haven't trained properly for nearly a week.'

'You have a programme?' she asked curiously.

'A rigorous one,' he said ruefully. 'Unrelenting. I need to be fit for what I do.'

'Running from the law?' she suggested, a light laugh hiding her bitterness.

'Tramping through jungles,' he corrected drily. 'Wandering across mountains. I like to work hard but I play hard too. It's good to balance the world of negotiations and wheeler-dealing with physical hardship. I got lost in a blizzard in Tibet once,' he confided. 'A bad lapse of concentration.' He frowned. 'I'd heard some bad news,' he muttered.

'What happened?' she asked.

He shrugged. 'It made me angry enough to fight for survival. For two days I kept my sanity by remembering every detail of our childhood adventures. By the time I'd reached the moment when I first kissed you, I was quite enjoying trudging along, reminiscing.' He smiled. 'Then when I discovered I'd judged my whereabouts correctly and came across my companions I was actually rather annoyed!'

She laughed, utterly fascinated. 'What were you all doing in Tibet?' she asked.

'Freezing!' he grinned. 'It was a well-earned holiday. It was wonderful.'

He bent his head and kissed her, catching her hand again and forcing her to run back up the steep slope with him to the house. Breathless, she felt herself being pushed indoors and up the stairs, half laughing with exhilaration.

In fern-green leotard and cotton-velvet tracksuit, she jogged up and down, waiting for Ruan in the hall. When he appeared, she looked at him from beneath her lashes, devouring the contours of his body as he ran lightly down the stairs. And in silent companionship they raced along the path to the beach in the clean, crisp air, pounding along together as if they'd never left one another.

'I can't go much further!' she gasped, when they'd toiled up the killing ridge of Windmill Hill.

Ruan slowed his relentless pace, his face bathed in sweat, like hers. 'You mean you admit that I have more stamina than you?' he teased.

She glared and set her teeth. 'You won't beat me!' she declared.

'Oh, I think I will,' he murmured.

She flashed him a suspicious look, but he was grinning crookedly, apparently amused by her grim determination. 'At least it's downhill most of the way back,' she panted.

'No. We're going up. I have another surprise,' he said, flashing her a grin. 'Over here. I have lunch waiting.'

Warily she watched him vault a gate and hold out his arms to her invitingly. 'Lunch?' she frowned. 'You've set up a picnic?'

He smiled enigmatically and she climbed the gate, allowing him to lift her down. And to kiss her. She wrapped her arms around his neck, too exhausted and weak to waste energy refusing him.

'Nice appetiser,' he murmured, his eyes glowing. He licked the salty sweat on her cheekbones and the warm rasp of his tongue was intensely erotic. She panted heavily and his mouth enclosed hers, his probing tongue seeking its inner moisture till she could bear no more and drew away.

'Lunch?' she queried hopefully, her gravelly voice betraying the effect he'd had on her.

'We need transport. Something other than our four feet.'

His eyes were laughing at her with such happy secrecy that she couldn't help but laugh back and let him lead her over the field. Cattle had been trampling the grass by the open gate, leaving an area of mud.

'Do we have to go over this?' she asked doubtfully.

'I don't have a cloak to do my Sir Walter Raleigh bit,' he grinned. 'So...' Ruan picked her up and held her close to his chest, striding into the next field, and she felt the heavy beat of his heart against her body and her hands splayed out in pleasure, feeling his warmth through the thin shirt. 'Oh, look,' he said in feigned surprise. 'A balloon. How opportune. We have transport!'

Diverted from gazing up at his face, she jerked her head around in alarm. 'Oh, no, Ruan!' she protested, seeing his intention. 'You've obviously planned this surprise very carefully, but I'm not going in that.' The basket lay on its side and the scarlet balloon was almost fully inflated, two men holding the opening while Caroline directed the jet from the burners into the envelope. 'You know I get vertigo!' she said crossly, wriggling in his arms. They tightened and a quiver of fear passed through her mind. 'What are you doing?' she said anxiously.

'You'll love it,' he assured her. 'Morning, Caroline,' he said cheerfully. 'I thought you would have given in your notice by now.'

'It's on your desk,' Caroline said wryly. 'Trust you to guess. I suppose you know me pretty well by now,' she added, as the two men righted the basket. 'David and I are discussing one or two things and when I get back from London——'

'Don't explain. It's not necessary,' said Ruan, quite unconcerned. 'I wish you well. Chocks away.'

He dumped the bewildered Natasha inside the deep wicker basket and leapt in, pulling on a lever. Before she knew what was happening, they were rising into the air. She stood petrified with fear. And then, when she saw how far away the ground was, her knees gave way and she collapsed in a heap on the floor, her eyes wide with terror.

'Take me down!' she yelled hysterically.

'In about half an hour or so,' he soothed.

'Half——? I can't stand it that long!' she croaked, furious that he was making her suffer. 'You know I hate heights!' she said furiously. 'You *know*! You got me down from the cliff when I froze. You talked me down. You were *nice*!' she wailed. 'Turn back!'

'I can't. You never can, Natasha,' he said quietly. 'That's why it's so important to select the right course in the first place.'

'Which is?' she asked sullenly, certain he meant more than choosing where his wretched balloon was going.

'Put this on.' He held out a luxuriously padded jacket.

'I'm not cold,' she said, surprised at the fact.

'You will be. You're cooling down from running. Here.'

She had to half rise to put her arms into the cosy jacket. While she was in that position, she cautiously peered out. 'How clear everything is!' she cried, holding her leaping stomach tightly.

Sunlight was bouncing off the angles of the waves in Gerrans Bay. Below lay the Roseland peninsula, green, undulating, divided by deeply wooded river valleys, the bare branches of the trees shining a rich cinnamon and gold. Cattle ran below them with a thudding that she could hear clearly, pheasants flew, startled from copses, and people waved from a farmhouse garden. She waved back cautiously. A startling blast from the burners sounded loud near her head and she popped down again.

'Why isn't it windy?' she asked, flushing at Ruan's chuckle.

'Because you travel with it—unless you hit an airstream which follows a river or a gorge.' He sighed contentedly. 'I love being up here. Makes you feel at one with the world,' he said happily.

'Why are you doing this to me?' she muttered.

'People pay good money for this,' he chided. 'I thought it would give us some time together, to be honest. And it's good to see things from another perspective. There,' he said, pointing, before she could question his meaning. 'Oh, do stop scrabbling on the floor and come up. I'll hold you safely. Come and see.' Slowly she rose, to be enfolded safely in his arms. 'Don't look down, sweetheart, look across,' he said in her ear. 'Less frightening.'

'Nice,' she admitted, after one long, nervous look. The tranquillity, the early morning sunshine made the countryside glisten, the streams and rivers sparkling like diamonds as they snaked their way to the sea. It was enchanting. 'The silence up here is extraordinary. As if the world's holding its breath. It's all very calm,' she marvelled, standing a little straighter. 'And yet exhilarating at the same time.'

He gently extracted one hand and fired the burner again. 'Perfect, isn't it? You'd never imagine you could get a combination of serenity and excitement,' he smiled, kissing her forehead. 'I took Winifred up once. She was thrilled.'

Natasha forgot her fear. 'Winifred?' she repeated in surprise. 'In a hot-air balloon? When?'

'Oh, after you left, I came back to see her in the home a few times. I'd tell her about the places I'd seen and give her the odd present from my travels. I got very fond of her. And very protective,' he said quietly, his eyes watchful.

Her face gentled. Ruan had some good in him. 'She thought the world of you,' she recalled warmly. 'Odd that she's gone elsewhere, isn't it? I meant to ask David why she'd been moved. After all, she loved being taken around Falmouth shopping, and she knew all the other residents so well.' A frown puckered her brow. 'She can't have made the decision to go; she wasn't capable of that,' she said slowly. 'So someone must have made it for her—though I know she had no family.'

'It's very strange,' agreed Ruan, suddenly very relaxed. 'Find out for me if David knows where she is, will you? I'd like to see her again if she's still alive. But don't tell him it's for my information. He'd never tell you. And you wouldn't like me to lose contact with Win, would you?' He smiled winningly.

'No. I wouldn't,' she agreed.

She leant against Ruan as they drifted over the Cornish countryside, no longer feeling as if her stomach had dropped out. He held her safe, as he'd always done in the past; whenever she had attempted anything new like swimming to Black Rock or riding a bike, he'd been there, steadying her, encouraging her. And with Winifred and the old ladies in the home he'd been gentle and patient—far more so than anyone, including herself. 'They're missing out on life,' he'd said with a passion that had surprised her. 'And life is so exciting. They may not be able to experience it first hand any longer, but I can bring life to *them*.' And he had, regaling them all with stories of his adventures and escapades till everyone, including the staff, had been in fits of laughter.

A different perspective . . .

'You can be extraordinarily kind and generous,' she mused absently, voicing her thoughts aloud. 'Always helping the underdog.'

'And David?' he murmured, giving her a friendly squeeze. 'Is he kind and generous?'

She stared thoughtfully at the herd of softly lowing cattle below. She couldn't think of a single occasion when he'd shared anything. Ruan had always offered his meagre picnic around, stood his round of drinks, spent his hard-earned cash on little surprises for her.

'He sent me flowers for my birthday,' she said loyally, remembering with some guilt how she'd hated the stiff, gaudy and rather formal bouquets which had been made up in some anonymous shop.

'Would you have liked me to do that?' Ruan asked curtly.

'Oh, no!' she beamed, caught off-guard. 'I loved the flowers you brought every week. I knew you'd got up at the crack of dawn and scoured Tredinnick for them. Snowdrops and primroses, daffodils and cherry blossom, rhododendrons and azaleas, wild roses and foxgloves. Heavenly,' she sighed, a glorious smile transfixing her face.

'Winifred liked them too,' mused Ruan, his face shuttered.

'I was sorry that David was never interested in the elderly ladies,' she said slowly. 'When I was doing Winifred's hair, or you were entertaining everyone, he always sat in the office, studying the books.'

'Studying form,' muttered Ruan cynically.

Her eyes became troubled. 'You're convinced that he's brought pressure to bear on the residents so that they leave him bequests in their wills, aren't you?'

'It's a little more than that,' he answered gently. 'Find out where Winifred is for me and I'll tell you.'

'But——' she protested.

'I want to see her,' he said. 'Now let me concentrate on landing.'

Gradually the balloon lost height and she became fascinated in watching how Ruan played the wind, using a fine control of the burners to maintain the height he wanted. From his flight bag he took his radio telephone and called up his crew, who claimed to have a visual fix. Natasha's brain buzzed. She hadn't known it was that easy to follow a balloon.

'Have they been following us?' she frowned.

'Yes. It's not difficult,' he answered, only half attending. 'They can see us for miles.'

'Really? Why did Caroline make such a hash of it, then?'

He stiffened and Natasha knew with a sinking feeling that her suspicions had been right. His hesitation had been a fraction too long before he began to speak. 'Well, she——'

'Everything was carefully arranged, wasn't it?' she exclaimed angrily. 'You did intend to land at Penmellin, Caroline deliberately got "delayed"—and pretended that the Land Rover had broken down.'

'OK. So it was arranged to the last detail,' he agreed calmly, his eyes intent on the fields ahead.

She rounded on him furiously. 'You schemer! And why did you search my luggage?'

'I wondered if you had Winifred's address—or David's,' he frowned. 'You returned the compliment, didn't you? You saw my map with Penmellin marked as my put-down point.'

'Yes,' she snapped. 'Why did you land there?'

'Because I knew you'd be there and I wanted to arrange a meeting,' he said quietly. 'I'd called at the home to see Winifred and discovered she'd been moved. I talked to the matron—she had no idea where Winnie had gone but she was full of David's venture, your return, everything.'

'So you pretended to make an emergency landing.'

His alert eyes scanned the field ahead. 'Yes. I thought I might stop you from doing something you'd regret. I didn't want you mixed up with David.'

'That you made very clear,' she said scornfully. 'Has Caroline deliberately set out to seduce David? If so, I'll let him know——'

'She has, but that was her own decision, not my instructions,' Ruan answered. 'She's pretty quick off the mark when it comes to rich pickings. I suppose she decided there wasn't any hope where I was concerned. She knew I wanted to see you again.'

'That's what you think I want to hear,' she said bitterly.

'No. It's true. I've missed you,' he told her, the simple truth quite clear in his frank eyes. 'I've missed you very much.'

'You've . . . *missed* me?' she whispered.

'You and Roseland. My heart's here,' he said quietly.

'But——'

'Crouch on the floor. Back to the direction we're travelling in. Do it!' She obeyed hastily and he relaxed. 'Hold the rope loops and brace yourself.'

'Oh, God! Are we going to crash?' she asked, going white.

'No, no,' he said in a calm, reassuring tone. 'It's a precaution. People think I'm reckless but you can be absolutely sure that I'm very, very careful in everything I do. Hold on.'

He was silent for a moment and Natasha waited for the bump and the collapse of the envelope on top of them. Her mouth drooped. She didn't want to struggle with Ruan under a sheet of scarlet silk again.

'How long?' she asked nervously, screwing up her face.

'We've landed, sweetheart.'

She looked up. Ruan was gazing at her with an expression of faint amusement. Above them, the balloon billowed full of air as it had before. With great care, she peered over the edge of the basket and saw grass. And they were firmly perched on it.

'We're down! I never felt a thing!'

'I should hope not. I'm a brilliant pilot. Just a moment; we'll lift off again a little bit and drive over nearer to the gate and save the Land Rover cutting up the farmer's field.'

To her astonishment, he did exactly that, his skill filling her with admiration. Then, when they were stationary again, the realisation of what she'd done suddenly hit her. Amazement lit her face and then relief, followed by an uncontrollable urge to shout with glee.

'I did it!' she cried in elation. 'I did it, I did it! Isn't that terrific? Me, frightened of heights! Up—how high?'

'Unfortunately we didn't make the mile-high club,' he grinned. 'The journey was too short. About a thousand feet.'

'Wow!' she breathed. 'I feel I could conquer the world!'

'Hang on there,' chuckled Ruan, his eyes as bright as hers. 'Conquer it after I've taken this bottle of whisky to the farmer.'

'What...? You can't go—no!' she cried in horror, watching him jump out of the basket and begin to stride away. 'Ruan!' she squeaked, glancing nervously up at the softly billowing balloon. 'Don't leave me! I'm not that brave!'

'It won't move——'

'Throw out sandbags or something! Anchors! Please, you can't leave me here! Come back!'

Chuckling, he returned to kiss her thoroughly. 'It'll stay here quite safely.' But she clung in fear and he laughed, lifting her out of the high basket, sliding her slowly down the length of his body. And he was aroused, his eyes telling her so, his mouth, his hands, his body insisting on showing her. 'If the farmer weren't on his way, and the retrieve crew as well, I'd take you right now,' he growled, panting heavily.

And she would have let him, she thought, driven by the exhilaration and the adrenalin surging through her body and Ruan's agonisingly sweet words: *'I missed you.'*

At midnight, she was curled up in the back of a taxi in Ruan's arms, sleepily listening to his recollection of the days they'd spent playing crazy games in Tredinnick's garden. She felt warm, comfortable and drowsy after the long, exhausting day. He'd been a different person, considerate, affectionate, fun to be with. The Ruan she'd known of old. The Ruan she'd loved.

It wasn't hard to believe that he half loved her now, the way he had behaved. After champagne and sandwiches in the field, they had just wandered around the lanes hand in hand, sometimes chatting like old friends, or in a peaceful silence. They'd watched the sunset stain the sky a peachy pink and then a dusky violet, sitting by a tidal mill-pool, straining their eyes till the black lace silhouettes of the trees had merged in with the blackness. When she'd said she was hungry again, Ruan had led her unerringly into a village and its pub.

She sighed. 'I've enjoyed today. I'll always remember it. Thank you for taking me flying,' she said dreamily.

'Everyone should fly once in their lives,' he murmured in her ear. 'Everyone should reach for the stars.'

'Yes, but I need you along for that,' she began, then trembled at what she'd said. 'I meant,' she said hastily, 'that I couldn't fly without you——'

'I know,' he said gently. 'I know that.'

Her heart thudded and she shot him an anxious glance. Would he realise that she could never find her own heaven without him? 'Ruan,' she began, trying to change the subject. But her voice didn't sound normal.

'My darling,' he murmured. 'My darling Tasha.'

The words were too seductive. She abandoned herself to him. It was all she wanted. She loved him, whatever he did, whoever he was. Her heart soared as she admitted this to herself and she felt free as a bird, as free as she'd felt that afternoon, flying so silently over her beloved countryside.

'Ruan,' she whispered passionately. 'Oh, Ruan, Ruan, Ruan!'

'Oh, sweetheart,' he groaned. 'I want you to love me.'

'I——'

He smiled at her stricken face and gently caressed her face. 'Take the risk,' he whispered emotionally.

'I can't pretend, can I?' she said jerkily. His eyes blazed with a dazzling joy and she felt her heart swell in her breast. Overcome with emotion, she leant forward to kiss him with a passion that she'd never known she possessed. 'I love you,' she said fervently. 'I always have. I always will.'

His arms tightened in a hard band around her. 'Then don't throw yourself away on a man like David.'

Inside, she felt a sour sensation deflate her bubbling happiness. Was this why he'd taken her out and entertained her? Had he talked her into committing herself because all he wanted was the pleasure of taking her from the man he hated? She lay quiescent in his arms while he kissed her and all the time she felt a bitter-sweetness within her, because she knew these moments were only stolen and they would not last.

'It's years since I kissed a girl in a taxi,' he murmured softly.

Jealousy scoured a cruel path through her body. 'Who was the last?' she asked, unable to stop herself.

'Some blonde.'

Natasha waited, hoping he'd remember the time when they'd been so wrapped up in each other's arms that the taxi driver had patiently waited, allowing them to run up a bill far beyond the contents of Ruan's pocket, and only his charm had talked them out of paying the high fare. But he said nothing. He'd forgotten, she thought sadly, in the welter of women who'd followed her.

'We're almost there,' she said, disappointment in her voice.

'Yes.' He smiled enigmatically at her. 'Almost there.' He leaned back and let her check her hair. 'It's taken us long enough. Don't forget, I'm relying on you to get that information about Winnie.'

'All right.' It seemed unimportant. It wouldn't harm David in any way. She put her hand to her head, tension suddenly producing a fierce pain at the back of her skull.

'You look white. What's the matter?' he asked in concern.

'Headache,' she grimaced.

'Darling.' He cradled her in his arms and told the driver to go carefully around the last few corners. At the house, he waved the anxious Mrs Dawkins away and insisted on carrying her indoors and to her room. 'What can I do to help?' he asked, drawing the curtains and lighting a candle, so that her eyes weren't hurt by harsh light.

'Nothing,' she said in a dull voice.

'You doubt my motives,' he said quietly, his eyes shrewd.

'Is it any wonder, when you admit you've deceived me all along the line? I just don't know whether I'm coming or going,' she complained.

'Think of what we were to one another, before other people interfered and ruined our lives,' he murmured, smoothing her brow with his gentle hands.

'I daren't,' she breathed fretfully.

'Try. Can a man change that much?' He held her hand, his soothing voice relaxing her.

'You keep threatening me——'

'I'd do anything to rattle your brain,' he said quietly. 'Turn you upside-down, kiss you stupid, get you drunk— anything. I don't know what I have to do to persuade you that you've come to all the wrong conclusions and that your judgement of me hurts me more than you can ever know.'

Her huge eyes were fixed on him, solemn and uncertain. 'I want to believe you,' she said slowly. 'Believe me, I do! But I don't want to be hurt again.'

'Neither do I,' he murmured. 'Will you suspend all judgement for a while? I think I can prove myself to you—if you promise not to listen to anything David has to say about me.'

'What is it with you and David?' she asked quietly. 'He idolised you——'

'He's always hated me,' frowned Ruan. 'It took a while for me to discover that, but by then he'd arranged a reputation for me that no one doubted. I was the one who got blamed for anything that went wrong at school, remember? Mischief in the village, torched fields, vandalised phone boxes... Did you ever imagine I'd damage the environment I felt so passionately about?'

'You were careless; you'd dropped things which identified you——'

'Me? Careless?'

She bit her lip. No one could ever accuse him of that fault. He always paid attention to detail. 'You think someone planted the stuff?'

'David.'

'How can you be sure of that?' she asked, an unpleasant feeling inside her. 'I don't like hearing this, Ruan,' she said unhappily.

'I don't like saying it. I want to be relaxing you, soothing your headache, healing our friendship. But I can't stand by while you let him fool you too. David's rotten, through and through. He's envious, lazy, proud, greedy and consumed with lust for you.'

Her thoughts raced. Ruan was accusing David of the same sins he'd been saddled with. 'Ohhh! I hate all this conflict!' she moaned. A spasm of pain racked her and she felt herself being lifted against Ruan's comforting chest.

'I wish I could take away your headache,' he said helplessly.

'I wish you could,' she whispered. 'And my doubts, too.'

'I'll stay till you're asleep,' he said huskily. 'Give me a little more time. I'm going to bring it all to a swift end. I can't continue with this slow progress. I can't bear seeing you so distraught. You've softened me, Tasha. My resolve is melting.'

She felt too weak to demur though she was filled with foreboding about what he might be planning. 'I hope you mean that. I didn't like you hard and cold, like granite,' she mumbled.

He held her close and, if her instincts were anything to go by, then he was genuinely concerned for her welfare. The trouble was that she wanted him to be telling the truth so badly that she had no idea if her intuition could be trusted.

'Love me?' he crooned.

'Yes,' she said hopelessly. 'Yes.'

CHAPTER EIGHT

NATASHA awoke in the night and found that Ruan was still lying beside her, fast asleep. Tenderly she studied his slumbering face, which seemed for this moment to be as gentle and as effortlessly heartbreaking as she remembered from their carefree teenage days. Her finger stretched out to touch his thick, dark lashes and she traced the faintly fluttering crescents in awe.

'Don't betray me,' she whispered. 'Don't ever betray me.'

Her mouth moved over his drowsy lips and she felt the rasp of his darkening beard graze her face. And when she woke again it was to discover that he was leaning on one elbow, watching her intently as if he'd learn all her secrets by doing so.

'I slept better than I have for years,' he smiled. 'Come here.'

'You're all bristly,' she complained happily into his warmly moving mouth.

He stroked his jaw ruefully. 'Nag, nag, nag!' he teased. 'OK. I'll shave. When I come back, I'll have a list of activities for today. That is presuming you don't want to spend it in bed with me?'

She hastily drew the bedclothes up to her eyes. 'No!' she said hastily.

'A man can hope,' he said sadly, but smiled to allay her fears. 'Kidding, sweetheart. You've got fifteen minutes.'

Natasha jumped up the moment he'd gone, hurtling in for a quick shower. Nervously towelling herself dry, she hunted through her clothes for something to wear.

Not the pink. Not a suit. Not her blue... She glanced at her watch and panicked. Eight minutes and she wanted to look wonderful! Where had the time gone? Two minutes for underwear and a flattering cream dress that made her eyes look startlingly wide; three to brush her hair furiously so that the static electricity made it fly into thick, face-framing ripples and gave her the appearance of a Renaissance princess; three to moisturise her face and slowly, carefully accentuate her eyes and tint her mouth with Fondé's new lip-enhancer.

Excited, glowing, she rushed to the door.

'Took you long enough.'

She grinned at the nonchalant Ruan, waiting outside, dressed in a dazzling green jacket and grey cords. 'Where did you get that?' she giggled.

'Uruguay. It gave the parrots hysterics. I think it had certain mating qualities——'

'Not for me it hasn't,' she said sternly.

'Pity. You look absolutely *edible*.'

She laughed, delighted that he appreciated her efforts, and that they were friends again. It was more than she'd dared to hope. Desire was wonderful. Friendship took it deeper.

'Where's this list of events, then?' she asked shyly.

He tapped his head. 'In here. Breakfast in the attic first.'

'In the *where*?' she asked, askance.

'Attic. Mrs Dawkins was a bit surprised too. I said we were re-living childhood memories and she went all soft and kissed me,' he said smugly. 'I think I've scored.'

It rained that day, the vicious Atlantic gales driving torrents of horizontal rain across the subtropical gardens and hurtling salt-laden water at the windows with a tremendous force. The storm, however, only emphasised the security and comfort of the solidly built house. And their contentment together.

Much to Ruan's delight, the electricity failed, and in the winter gloom they spent a happy time fooling around with only the glow of golden candles to soften the velvety darkness.

'Please, Ruan, I'm aching,' she wailed, weakly collapsing into a drawing-room armchair, as he tried unsuccessfully to pot a chickpea into an egg-cup with a warped billiard cue.

He sighed, ceased his hilarious commentary, and came to sit at her feet. 'Almost time for David to come home,' he said, sobering with a chilling suddenness.

She tried not to wish they had the house to themselves. They'd avoided David that morning by eating in the attic, but sooner or later she knew she'd have to face up to the fact that there was rift between the two men that would never be healed. And she refused to think about the future of her relationship with Ruan.

'I'll find a time to get him on his own and broach the subject of Winifred,' she said quietly.

'Please.' Ruan touched her knee in gratitude. She stroked his hair and he reached back for her hand to kiss it. 'I want to tell you about her,' he said. 'I don't like keeping secrets from you any more. I've just got used to keeping my thoughts and feelings private.'

'I know. I think you really began to draw away from us all when your father died,' she said compassionately. 'You forced yourself to grow up fast. You drove yourself to achieve all those terrible, impossible goals you set yourself. And you slowly shut us all out in the process.'

'I had to pay back every penny of my debts,' he said quietly. 'I owed that to my mother and my father's memory. And I wanted to prove to everyone that I could run a business—and do it honourably.'

'You worked too hard. I wish you had taken it more slowly and we hadn't been estranged,' she said earnestly.

'Sweetheart, I worried about getting too close to you. I knew I would have to go away from Roseland to make my fortune,' he said in a low tone. 'Your mother convinced me that it was better for you if I didn't ask you to wait for me. She'd done so much waiting of her own and her life had virtually ended when your father died. I know the pain she suffered. It seemed better for you to end the relationship before we'd really committed ourselves to one another.'

'You didn't feel you could rely on my loyalty? That I might be able to help you in your work?' she asked, hurt.

'You were very young and you'd never had another boyfriend,' he said gently. 'I thought you should spread your wings a little. And you didn't quite trust me, did you?'

Her brow furrowed and he smoothed it out with his firm fingertips. 'I was so unsure of myself. I didn't believe you loved me,' she said huskily.

'God!' he growled. 'I still don't know if I should get involved with you again!'

'Why? Because you live outside the law? Because you will always want to risk your life?' she asked miserably. 'Why don't you want to settle down? I almost wish you watched television endlessly, like David!' she said, her mouth pouting in sullen resentment.

'Slippers and pipe? Sex on Saturday night, bingo on Thursdays?' Ruan pulled her down to the floor beside him and kissed the pout away. 'You forget, I tried to settle down once. I tried to build up a business that would give me excitement and interest yet keep me in the area I loved above all.'

'You're accusing me again of spoiling your dreams! But I didn't mean to hurt you!' she sobbed. 'It was the last thing I wanted to do! I loved you!'

'I know,' he soothed. 'I know.' He held her in a grip of iron and she was glad of the pain. Her desperately unhappy eyes meshed with his and she saw such tenderness in their dark warmth that she felt her whole body shudder.

'Ruan,' she breathed, letting herself melt into him.

'Don't doubt me, darling.'

'I won't!'

Gently he laid her down, his eyes blazing with vibrance. Her arms reached around his back, automatically massaging it. He groaned. 'Oh, that's good!' he breathed.

'I'll do it properly,' she said huskily, wanting to please him. 'I'll need oils. Wait while I get them. Take your jacket off.' She took a deep breath. 'And your shirt.'

When she returned, Ruan had stretched comfortably in front of the roaring log fire. A little apprehensively, Natasha tipped one of the potent phials into her cupped palms, waiting till the warmth of her skin released the sensual aromas. Her mouth went dry as she knelt and reached forward to begin, the candle-light flickering on his naked back.

Her expert fingers worked up the smooth, honey-gold skin each side of his spine and across his shoulders, easing out the knots. For a supposedly laid-back man, he was very tense. She would almost have thought he lived on his nerves, the way his body tightened up when she touched it.

'Relax,' she ordered, trying to sound professional.

'I can't,' he muttered.

She grasped the shoulder muscle and squeezed out the tension. As she moved deeper into the massage, he began to respond. His body first, the muscles easing with the constant, rhythmical touch, his nostrils assailed by the same erotic perfume that was making her muscles weak too. Then he began to murmur his pleasure, small grunts, sighs, long groans.

She'd worked on men before, during her training course. None had made her feel so burning hot. None had made her loins ache with need when she stroked his pliant body, nor had she felt a sense of hesitant delight when she'd touched him—an almost electric tingle in her fingertips. And seeing Ruan respond so sensually to her hands gave her a thrill so intensely carnal that it shocked her.

'You're tightening up again,' she whispered, her heart thudding with the movement of her fingers, slowing now, on the glorious stretch of his back.

He rolled over and she recognised the light of desire glowing in his eyes and the sultriness of his slightly parted mouth. 'It's not surprising,' he said thickly. His hand caressed her breast and it was so ready for his touch that she gave a sharp cry as it swelled before her eyes.

She bent her head and boldly, before she knew what she was doing, encircled his nipple with her mouth in an exploratory move that sent shudders through his body. Her breathing quickened.

'I think——'

'Don't,' he groaned. 'No thinking. I want to touch you.'

Gently he unzipped her dress, kissing her with such restrained passion that she felt no fear. And suddenly she wanted to be naked, to lie against his body and to feel her heated skin on his.

Lying close together, entwined, stroking and touching, she felt a slow fire building inside her. And her trust in him was so powerful now that she wanted him to quench it.

'You're beautiful,' he murmured huskily, his voice shaking with passion. 'More beautiful, more desirable than I could ever have imagined.' His fingers swooped over her body and it was all sensation; she gave a low cry and abandoned herself utterly to him, fiercely running her hands to all but the secret place which she dared not touch. Yet.

He hugged her, reassuring her. And she closed her eyes in pure ecstasy as he lovingly caressed the moist core of her body. 'Oh, Ruan!' she gasped. 'It's wonderful! It feels ... I didn't know...'

'He-e-e-ll!' he grated jerkily.

She felt his fingers slide reluctantly away. With difficulty, she focused. 'What's the matter?' she mumbled indistinctly.

'Tasha.' His agonised face swam into view. 'Has...has any man touched you like that before?' he asked in a choked voice.

She shook her head dumbly, coming back from the edge of paradise. 'Not ... there.' Her breath shuddered in. 'You—you only like experienced women?' she whispered. The pulses in her body screamed for release, sending her crazy. 'I'll learn! Oh, God, Ruan! Teach me!' she cried, hardly knowing what she was saying.

He held her fiercely. 'I will,' he said grimly. 'I will. Not now.'

To her dismay, she felt him roll away. 'What have I said?' she asked in horror. 'It's happening again—you——!'

'No. You've said nothing wrong.' He was dressing fast as if the Furies were after him. Then he paused, and took a deep breath. 'It was my fault,' he said hoarsely. 'I never imagined...Tash, I have to leave you.'

'Because you've had your day's entertainment?' she asked wildly. 'You got me to bed, like an adoring little dog——?'

'Stop it!' His hand slapped his forehead hard. 'Don't *do* this to me!' he yelled. 'Oh, damn it!' He knelt and wiped away the tears that were springing into her eyes. 'Sweetheart, you don't know much about men,' he said wryly.

'You want me to go and learn?' she asked crossly.

'I'd kill the man who touched you,' he said with soft savagery. 'I want you like mad. I'd like nothing better than to make love to you. Now. And again. And again, and again!' He sighed at her bewildered, tear-stained face and kissed where the tears ran, making her shudder and sob.

'Then—why?' she wailed.

'Hush,' he soothed, rocking her tenderly. 'It's because you are a virgin. I'm not going to take you.'

'Someone has to! The human race would end if everyone felt that way! You've got something against them?' she asked resentfully.

He laughed with affection and kissed her moist nose. 'I admire them. I respect them,' he told her seriously. 'I admire and respect you. However, there's something I have to do before... Tasha, I'm not entirely free——'

'Oh, God! You're married!' she gasped in panic.

He smiled. 'No, darling. But I want to take you freely, without any barriers between us. When I can offer you...' He frowned. 'What am I saying? You make me talk too much,' he scolded.

'I wish I knew what you were talking *about*,' she sighed.

'I care for you,' he said quietly. 'So much that I'll deny myself the chance to take what I've wanted for years. Here you are, here I am, and we are both ready to make love. I swore to have you, remember?'

Her eyes rounded. 'What...?'

'Isn't this proof that I'm thinking of you and not myself?' he asked gently. 'For your sake, I'm exerting a little self-discipline. I'm going away for a while to cool down. Don't doubt me. Do you hear?' he added in a fierce voice. 'For God's sake, don't doubt me!'

'Kiss me,' she said anxiously.

He groaned and did so. As they clung together, she realised how tense and how aroused he was and it awed her that he should hold back for her sake. Later, she thought contentedly, reassured by his repeated, adoring kisses. He would love her properly later.

* * *

'Have you been in my study?'

She looked up to see an irate David blocking the drawing-room doorway. 'No,' she replied, frowning. 'Why would I want to?'

'Someone's removed a file from my cabinet,' he barked.

'Not me. Has Mrs Dawkins been cleaning in there?'

'No one goes in there,' snapped David. 'I keep it locked.'

'Well,' she smiled, relaxing, 'you've just mislaid it, then.'

'Or Ruan's taken it. Where is he?' he asked.

Her smile broadened dreamily. 'He can't have taken your file. He's in Truro,' she said softly. 'He telephoned me a moment ago.'

'Huh!'

She blinked. David had flounced out and she hadn't even had a chance to ask him about Winifred.

It was two days since she and Ruan had come so close to making love, and her face still flushed to think about it. He'd kept in touch by telephone, four times the first day he was absent, four times yesterday, three times so far today, and she felt contented and cherished.

Happily she changed into her jogging-suit and set off for a run. She pounded down the rain-washed lane, which had been worn deep by donkeys carrying sacks of salted pilchards from Penmellin's fish cellars.

'I love Ruan, Ruan loves me!' she chattered happily, in rhythm to her feet. And then slowed. He'd never actually said that.

Natasha stood stock-still, intending to think this over, but a movement ahead distracted her and she saw Ruan himself, leaning against his car, talking to the revenue man who was presumably on his patrol. They seemed oddly familiar with one another as if they were old friends.

She pressed into the hedge, her thoughts diverted as the awful doubts began to surface. First, Ruan couldn't have been in Truro when he rang. Second, with his skill in breaking and entering, he could well have searched David's study and taken the file that David had seemed so worried about.

She gasped. A third reason had added itself to her list. Something suspiciously like money was changing hands between Ruan and the man. Bribing an official! She'd heard plenty of rumours in the past that occasionally a customs and excise man could be bribed to patrol another district while contraband was landed in one of Roseland's many secret creeks.

Distressed, she crept away till she was out of earshot, when she began to run as if the devil were after her. A car growled into life, smoothly accelerated, and she only had a few moments to prepare herself before Ruan appeared.

'Jump in, sweetheart! Surprised?'

'Stunned,' she retorted brightly, getting in and suffering his deceitful kiss. Her mind see-sawed like a child picking daisy petals. She loved him, she loved him not. She trusted him, she trusted him not.

'Got the Press coming,' he said. 'Thought I'd warn you to put on your best knock-em-dead outfit. Something classy. And prepare a few words of wisdom.'

'You don't believe in giving a girl much of a warning,' she complained, wishing she didn't have a Press call to worry about too.

'Sorry,' he said with a disarmingly apologetic smile. 'Things are happening faster than I'd planned.'

She let her head turn so that the wind blew her hair over her face and shielded her bitter expression. One thing at a time, she told herself. The PR work was very important.

'I think I can handle it,' she said distantly. 'Will they interview you too?'

'I'm playing a back-seat part,' he replied. 'You're so much prettier. I always avoid the Press, since that filthy article about me that David arranged to be plastered all over the local papers.'

More accusations. She forced a smile and used the excuse of preparing for the interview to avoid contact with Ruan when they arrived at the house, jumping out of the car and racing inside with a vague wave in his direction.

When she came down, it was to find a smartly dressed David supplying the reporters and photographers with champagne.

'Over here, darlin'!'

'On the stairs, hand on the dragon's head . . . lovely!'

Flashlights popped and she obligingly posed where the photographers asked, calmly and gracefully answering all the reporters' questions. Ruan was nowhere to be seen. Her heart thudded under her serene exterior, a sense of foreboding making it difficult for her to concentrate.

'Shall we go to the beauty salon?' beamed David, pleased with the way it was going.

Her nerves were jumping. It was all too smooth. Something would happen. She led the way, expecting Ruan to leap out and denounce them both at any moment. Her hand faltered on the door.

'Get a move on, darlin',' complained one of the reporters. 'Got another job this morn . . . Good God!'

Natasha stood immobile in the ruins of the room she'd so carefully arranged. Someone had wrecked it. Jars and creams lay scattered on the dove-grey carpet, oils seeping into the thick pile. The wickedly expensive curtains hung like rags, slashed beyond repair. And beyond, in the exercise-room, her horrified eyes saw that the equipment had been vandalised . . .

'Oh, you bastard!' she whispered.

'Oh, boy, some story!' cried the reporter.

She was shouldered aside. The flashlights filled the devastated rooms with blinding light, reporters scribbling furiously, pestering her with questions, hounding her into a corner where she stood white-faced and shaking, incapable of speaking.

'Natasha! *Natasha*!' Ruan's call made itself heard over the bedlam. 'Good grief!' he exclaimed, when he saw the damage. 'Who——?'

'*Who*? What do you mean, *who*?' she screamed, astounded at his gall.

He flashed a glance at David, his dark eyes hard and shrewd and filled with loathing. Then his mouth thinned to a determined line. 'Fraud squad's here,' he said loudly, as if announcing it to the whole room. 'Asking for David.'

'Fraud...!' Natasha couldn't believe her ears. Even the Press men were silent, breathlessly, eagerly awaiting developments.

'Ruan!' David said hoarsely. 'You conniving, cheating...! Wait till I get my hands on you!'

'Ruan who?' enquired a reporter solicitously.

'Gardini!' grated David. 'He'll be in your files. Associates with drug traffickers. That's him.' David's eyes lit up maliciously. 'He did this.'

Ruan turned quickly and ran along the corridor. 'Oh, no, no, no!' moaned Natasha, the tears falling unchecked down her cheeks.

There was no one to hear her. The room had emptied in seconds. She leaned against the door. Ruan had deliberately set out to wait till he had the opportunity for a maximum of publicity. The story would be plastered across the Dailies. FRAUD SQUAD INVESTIGATES BEAUTY CLINIC. It was doomed before it opened.

She groaned in despair. Yet... surely he'd lost all his credibility as Fondé's owner? He'd have to sell the company, she realised. A chill stole over her whole body. That was what he'd meant when he'd said he knew he was destroying himself too. He'd quite cold-bloodedly decided that, if necessary, he'd pay that penalty for the satisfaction of ruining her and David.

'My God!' she whispered. 'He's as hard as stone!'

Grimly she made her way to the sound of voices, trusting the reporters to have hunted Ruan out. She wanted to make the position clear and to have a showdown with him.

They were taking shots of the fraud squad—one of them, she vaguely registered, was oddly familiar. The men were carrying David's files through the battered door of his office. The Press excitedly followed the officials down the stairs and out to the waiting vans.

Her dead, darkened eyes met Ruan's. ' "Don't doubt me"!' she rasped bitterly, mocking the impassioned plea he'd made to her. ' "Sweetheart"!' she spat.

'Hold on,' he said in a low tone. 'David——'

'No,' she said, her head snapping up in anger. 'You! It's always been you, and you've laid the blame on him unfairly.' She heard David's feet thudding down the stairs and turned blindly to him. 'Hit him! Lay him out at my feet!' she urged, the sheer violence of her emotions making her hysterical. 'Do it, before I do!'

David ignored her challenge, staring wildly at Ruan. 'They've got my files. They'll find out!'

'Yes,' he said quietly, squaring up to the white-faced David.

'You bastard! You've beaten me again! I could murder you for that, Ruan!' seethed David. 'Always winning! What is it with you? Where's the fairness in life? You were so damn good at everything, so perfect——'

'No. Never that,' Ruan growled. 'But I practised. I fought like a dog for everything I've achieved.'

'Even Natasha?' asked David bitterly. 'You never had to bother. You had her without effort. I loved her! I always have! Why did she run after you as soon as she could toddle? I was better dressed, educated, from a better class! And still she tagged along behind you like the rest of the female hordes!'

'You'd do anything to get her, wouldn't you?' goaded Ruan.

'And so would you!' David countered.

'You pretended to be my friend, while all the time you were trying to blacken my name. You tampered with my sub-aqua equipment so the safety officer banned me from operating,' went on Ruan relentlessly. 'You did everything you could to make Natasha come running to you——'

'And I succeeded,' said David with a fierce pride. 'I beat you then, Ruan Gardini! She fell into my arms and I kissed her again and again!'

'Oh, no!' Natasha whispered. Betrayed, she thought. By the two men closest to her. David had planned Ruan's downfall. David. The man she'd turned to.

'The fraud squad are waiting to talk to you,' said Ruan evenly.

'They can wait forever. Your arrival put me on my guard. You made me take precautions against any eventuality,' breathed David. He turned to Natasha, his face hot and shiny. 'I have two tickets to take us a long way from here,' he said excitedly. 'Come with me—I have a hell of a lot of money in ready cash. You can live like a queen——'

'Or you can stay here and marry me,' said Ruan quietly.

Stunned at their preposterous suggestions, she looked from one to the other, her head hurting unbearably. She put a distracted palm to her ice-cold brow and her fingers felt the heavy pulsing at her left temple.

'Quick! Yes or no? I have to get clear of the revenue!'

'The...the revenue man!' Something clicked inside her head. 'You can relax, David,' she said, harsh and scathing. 'I doubt that those so-called officials really are what they pretend to be. One of them was out on the road being secretly bribed by Ruan this morning——'

'Oh, God!' Ruan groaned.

'It doesn't matter who they are; can't you see I can't stay?' cried David impatiently. 'My reputation will be ruined by the publicity! He's done to me what I did to...' David stopped, horrified at what he'd said.

'What you did to him?' whispered Natasha.

'I can explain everything. Come with me,' urged David.

'What,' she ground out, 'did you do to Ruan?'

'Only what he deserved for being so cock-sure,' said David curtly. 'Every day of my life I thought of ways to get even with him and I got him into trouble all along the line. I'm cleverer than he is, Natasha. Stick with me. You have to come with me; you have nothing here,' he said urgently. 'No job, no future. Tredinnick can't function as a beauty centre. You'll have to pay Fondé for all that ruined stock and equipment and the loan they gave me——'

'They gave you?' she gasped.

'Yes. You owe me a great deal of money,' said Ruan quietly.

'You smashed my salon——' she began heatedly.

Ruan glared. 'No. David did. So you'd lose thousands if you stayed. So you'd have no choice but to go with him.'

'Yes or no!' yelled David frantically.

'No! I don't want to. I don't love you, David; I don't like you!' she said in disgust, loathing them both equally.

The shock struck him dumb for a moment. 'But— but—I did all this for you!' he grated. 'Everything! I put my career on the line, schemed and worked so that I could shower you with money! You turn me down, you bitch? Well, I'm saving my own skin. Damn you both to hell!'

She clutched at the door-jamb, desperate for support as David raced to the back of the house. 'Where's he going?' she cried hoarsely.

Ruan's expression was grim. 'I suspect he'll head for that creek. There's a motorboat waiting there—but I know about that. I removed part of the engine. Poor Caroline. She had such high hopes.'

'He—he lied . . .' She gulped unhappily.

'You always had a blind belief in him,' said Ruan bitterly.

'I felt sorry for him. He couldn't compare with you——'

'But you trusted him and not me,' he said with quiet regret. 'You wouldn't believe me.'

'The man in the lane——!' she began hotly.

'Is what he appears to be. The local revenue man.'

'You bribed him——'

'How dare you think that of me?' he said angrily. 'They were my written notes with all the evidence needed to back up the raid they've just carried out. I've been trying all this time to get proof of the frauds that David's been pulling.'

'But what fraud? What exactly are the fraud squad doing here?' she asked, bewildered.

'Shutting down David's nasty scam,' he growled. 'I burgled his study.' Her eyes widened. 'I got the Press here and timed it so that the squad would arrive and David would never be able to practise again as a solicitor, or to hold a position of trust.'

'You vindictive swine!' she breathed. Cold inside, she walked stiffly to the stairs.

'Where are you going?' he asked quickly.

'To my room,' she said with dignity. 'To pack. I have to get away from you. You're trouble.'

'There's more. I think I'd better come clean,' he said quietly.

'There's too much mud sticking to you,' she snapped, beginning to ascend the stairs. 'As for the damaged stock and equipment, you damaged it, you pay for it.'

'There's no trust between us,' he said in a low tone.

'Is it surprising?' she cried, whirling to face him. 'You've got what you wanted—David's ruination, and presumably because of this loan you now own Tredinnick. Well, that's all you're getting. I'm not going to lie down and let you take your final revenge. I had such dreams for the clinic!' she continued passionately. 'I wanted us to subsidise people who couldn't afford treatment. I wanted to liaise with hospitals in the south-west, and help people——' She let out a loud cry of despair. 'Twice you've ruined my life!' she accused. 'I hope your sins will find you out!'

'Tasha——' he pleaded.

'No! You get out of my sight!' she yelled. 'Don't let me see you again this side of eternity, or I'll tear your evil heart out!' Sobbing bitterly, she ran like the wind to her room and slammed the door.

'Tasha!' he shouted, pounding on it with his fists. 'You're making a mistake——!'

'I made it long ago, when I didn't push you in the River Fal!' she yelled. 'Go away!'

'You haven't heard——'

'I've heard too much! I don't want to know that all men are liars, that I can't trust anyone!' she shouted.

'Damn you to hell!' he roared.

Natasha switched on her radio to full volume, blotting out his lies. She stared into space, the plaintively bawling love-song making her emotions boil over.

'Every step of the way,' she grated aloud, 'you've been there ahead of me, flattering, deceiving, concocting bare-faced *lies*!' She hurled the phone at the wall. Pillows. The bedside lamp. And flung herself across her bed to weep till the tears ran dry and the nightingale began to sing in the wild briar.

*   *   *

Six miserable months after Ruan had vanished that night she had found work in a hospital as a corrective cosmetic technician. Among the distressed burns patients, the facially scarred and the people recovering from plastic surgery her own anguish was lessened and in their gratitude she felt a little healed herself.

She sat in her little cottage one Saturday, a wild late spring storm tearing at its fabric. A sudden blast of wind howled into the room, causing chaos, and she jumped up to shut the window which had blown wide open.

But Ruan was already climbing through it.

'Get out!' she screamed hysterically, her hand on the telephone. 'Before I ring the police!'

He battled with the window and slammed it shut. 'No,' he said quietly.

'Get out, Ruan! There's a door—use it.'

'Not any more. I'm home.' He advanced on her and she nervously searched for somewhere to run. 'And you will listen to me, because you'll never forgive yourself if you don't know the whole story. Maybe you'll understand and pardon me for the deception,' he said softly.

'Never!' she insisted angrily, putting her hands on her ears.

He took them away. 'OK. But I have to try just this once more. Winifred,' he said sharply. 'You've read the report?'

'What report?' she asked sullenly.

'David's been charged with defrauding Winifred—and don't say you don't believe me,' he said, putting his hand over her ominously opening mouth, 'because it's here in this newspaper and the police have a watertight case.'

'How was he defrauding her?' she gasped.

'Winifred Tredinnick is a ward of the Court of Protection,' Ruan said gravely. 'A judge made her will, on her behalf, and appointed David as the receiver—that means he had full authority to handle her financial affairs. And he abused his position, going to live in

Tredinnick House—her house—borrowing money from me for the renovations till he could sell her shares, moving her money until great tranches of it had disappeared into his own coffers.'

Grimly he put the report in front of her and she read it. There were pictures of Winifred, smiling her sweet, contented smile, a small wooden model of St Mawes Castle in her hands. She groaned.

'That's the toy you found in David's attic!' she said slowly.

'Win was kept there for a while, to make her more difficult to trace,' said Ruan shortly. 'It meant there was a gap in her records and he was able to transfer her to somewhere cheap, further away, without anyone knowing where she'd gone.' His face darkened angrily.

'Poor Win,' she cried sympathetically.

He nodded. 'She was bewildered and unhappy when I tracked her down. You realise that she wasn't the only one David had screwed for cash. He'd made himself a fat income from the defenceless women in that nursing home of his.'

'This was why you came back? Why you hounded David so unmercifully?' she asked, beginning to understand.

'I was defending the defenceless,' he answered simply. 'When I discovered that Win had gone and David was showing signs of extravagance, I put two and two together. I've long been suspicious of his acquisitive nature. And then I heard you were returning, to work for David. I didn't know when I first arrived if you were involved or not. I *had* to be careful. I couldn't trust anyone.'

'Why did he ask me?' she frowned.

Ruan regarded her steadily. 'He's always wanted you. His desire was fanned into flames because of the old jealousy between us. Don't you know that he would have blackmailed you, claiming you were an accessory, if you'd stayed with him, and forced you to keep quiet?'

She shuddered. She heard the depth of passion vibrating through his body and knew he was telling the truth. 'You did this for Winifred, rather than to get your own back on David?'

'Yes. I'll always fight for the weak,' he agreed quietly. She hesitated and then came to stand a foot away, uncertain, unsure of herself. He smiled, with a sadness that touched her heart. 'Father told me when I was very young that strong men had a duty towards the weak.'

'Why didn't you tell me this six months ago?' she said brokenly.

'You just wouldn't have taken a blind bit of notice,' he said levelly. 'So I waited until I had proof, and here it is for you to see in black and white. I'm sorry you have such little faith in me. But now you know the truth and I can walk away and shut the book now that this chapter in my life has ended.'

'Oh, God!' she whispered. 'You're leaving? Because I believed everything David told me?' she said, appalled.

'You thought I was signalling to smugglers,' he said in a low tone. 'But I was only meeting people who'd sailed in to discuss a charter to the Channel Islands. There was a simple explanation. There always has been. You hurt me, Natasha.' Ruan went to the window, staring out at the wind which was lashing the water into creamy foam.

There was an awkward silence. 'Nothing—not anything wicked said about you was true,' she said huskily. 'Oh, Ruan, how tragic... You must have been so bitter——'

He shrugged his shoulders again, the back of his neck stiff with tension. 'You let me down,' he muttered. 'I have been deeply in love with you all my life.' He spun around on his heel, his face seething with passion. 'Why couldn't you see that? Why torture me with your doubts?

You made me shut out all love and tenderness so that I could survive.' He flinched a little at her shudder. 'I might seem tough, Natasha, but I'm flesh and blood, like you. I suffer too. I struggle and worry like the next person. The only difference is that I don't show it. But I loved you. Everything I did was for you. I tried to make you proud of me. To trust me. I wanted your love more than life itself.'

'Ruan!' she whispered. 'Don't let it end now! You were a ... a giant in my eyes, a god! I loved you so much that it hurt me physically, here in my breast. I never imagined you felt like this. I never believed that you could ever be satisfied only with me——'

'Of course I could!' he growled. 'Why don't you value yourself enough? If I could have had you...' He half turned, emotion claiming his voice.

'Yes, if?' she asked huskily.

'Don't you know that you could be four feet tall and five wide and I'd still love you?' he said passionately. 'Because it's a chemistry, a feeling, a crazy sensation that makes my heart lurch every time I see you! This is nothing to do with the fact that you're the most beautiful woman in the world, or that your nature is gentle and caring and... Oh, hell!' he muttered.

'Ruan,' she breathed, utterly shaken by his declaration.

'I made my fortune,' he said softly. 'I'm now free of the past with one exception. You. I don't want to walk away from you. But I will if you don't believe in me. You see, I want you, love you, will die loving you, Natasha.'

'After everything I've done? All the pain I've caused you?' she asked tenderly, her eyes shimmering with tears.

'Nothing matters, only love. And nothing will ever shake mine for you,' he said huskily.

The distance between them seemed to stretch forever. She wanted to cross it. Her throat constricted. Through a mist of tears, she saw his gentle smile when she took the first step. Her movement became more confident. Boldly she came to within inches of his tense body and tilted her pale, anxious face to his anguished, haunted eyes.

'You are the only man I can ever love,' she said simply. She saw him only dimly, the harrowing tears of emotion pouring down her face. 'I've misjudged you and despaired over you but I've never stopped loving you, Ruan,' she sobbed. 'I just never believed a man like you could feel deeply, permanently for someone as ordinary as me——'

'Not ordinary,' he whispered, the darkness of his eyes melting into hers. 'Never that. To me you have always been the first thing I think of when I wake, the last when I drift into sleep. And you've inhabited my dreams—especially these past few years—with devastating effect on my equilibrium,' he said wryly.

'Then we dreamed of one another,' she told him softly. Her smile made her eyes glow with happiness. 'Life without you is impossible. I don't care what your terms are; I'll live with you, marry you, go wherever you want. I just want to spend the rest of my life with you.'

His hands reached out shakily. A dazzling grin lit his face. He took her in his arms and held her, his palms firmly on her back, claiming her. It seemed that he was in no hurry to go further, just to feel her back where she belonged.

'We will do whatever *you* like, go wherever you like,' he murmured. 'Since I can live anywhere in the world, with all my financial interests and the ease of communication, you have the choice. But . . . ' He kissed her forehead gently. 'Would you like us to open up Tredinnick again?'

'Surely it belongs to Winifred's estate?' she reminded him.

'No. To me.' He smiled at her puzzled face. 'When the judge took evidence in his chambers from the staff at the home, they all said that she adored me——'

'She did,' interrupted Natasha warmly. 'You were son and father and brother and friend to her.'

'That's why the judge made me her sole beneficiary,' said Ruan. 'When she dies, I am to have Tredinnick. I saw a copy of the will and I've spoken to the judge. I have permission to bring her home. To Tredinnick. To make her life as rich as possible.'

'Oh, Ruan!' she cried, her eyes brilliant with happy tears. 'That's wonderful! I'm so glad!'

'Winnie is very wealthy,' he said soberly. 'The Tredinnicks made a fortune out of tin, as you know, and invested it well. I'd like us to spend our leisure time finishing the renovations on the house and garden. My dream is to make it a haven as you suggested —perhaps with you running the beauty clinic?'

'Can we extend the services of the clinic to the hospitals?' she asked anxiously, then told him about the work she'd been doing and what it meant to her.

'You're an angel,' he said approvingly. 'And as pure as the angels,' he added with a laugh.

'But—you'll be bored, living here——'

He shook his head, hugging her. 'I pretended I would, because that was the only way I could cope with the prospect of leaving Roseland—and you. In reality, it's what I've been longing to do all my life. And there'll be so much to do!' Gently he held her at arm's length. 'Marry me, my darling. Make it all a paradise on earth.'

She looked at him with adoration. 'Married!' she whispered. 'I can't believe——' His reproachful look stopped her from continuing and she laughed. 'OK, so I believe! Why should I be so happy?' she asked, quite bewildered.

'Because you deserve to be,' he murmured. 'We've both been through a terrible time but our love's survived it. Nothing can part us,' he whispered into her silken hair. 'Nothing.'

'It's going to be wonderful,' she marvelled breathlessly.

He held her without speaking for a long time, just holding her, looking dazed. And then he began to kiss her—slowly, sweetly, as if she were a tender flower he dared not injure. 'My darling,' he murmured huskily. She lifted sparkling eyes, as clear as the summer sea, her fingers gently resting on the firm contours of his heavily lurching chest.

'Take me to Tredinnick now,' she whispered.

'It's blowing a gale,' he protested gently.

'There's something we have to do there,' she said, her eyes like those of a mermaid tempting a sailor.

Tenderly he wrapped her up in a warm coat and tucked her up in his sleek car, driving with agonising care along the deep-cut lane. They both stared at Tredinnick House, knowing one day it would be theirs. And then Ruan gravely helped her out, enfolding her in his arms and shielding her from the howling wind that sought to tear them apart.

'Home!' she cried in joy, whirling around in the hall.

Ruan held out his arms to her. 'This is home,' he said. 'Wherever we are.'

She ran to him and he crushed her tightly to him. 'Light a fire for me in the drawing-room,' she murmured huskily.

Slowly, knowing his deep need for the tenderness of a woman's love, they undressed one another. They made love to one another by the glow of the sweet-smelling pine fire till finally they lay content and wrapped in each other's embrace.

She smiled to herself, playing with the lock of hair that curved on to his forehead, and he looked at her with a devotion that shook her to the core. There were no shadows or secrets in his eyes any longer.

Natasha stretched luxuriously and Ruan growled in his throat, running his hands over her voluptuous body. 'Darling,' she smiled. 'I'm so very happy.'

'God, how I love you!' he whispered, kissing her tenderly. 'I love you, Natasha, with every single beat of my heart.'

Take 4 bestselling love stories FREE

Plus get a FREE surprise gift!

Become a Privileged Woman,
You'll be entitled to all these *Free Benefits.*
And *Free Gifts,* too.

To thank you for buying our books, we've designed an exclusive FREE program called *PAGES & PRIVILEGES*™. You can enroll with just one Proof of Purchase, and get the kind of luxuries that, until now, you could only read about.

BIG HOTEL DISCOUNTS

A privileged woman stays in the finest hotels. And so can you—at up to 60% off! Imagine standing in a hotel check-in line and watching as the guest in front of you pays $150 for the same room that's only costing you $60. Your *Pages & Privileges* discounts are good at Sheraton, Marriott, Best Western, Hyatt and thousands of other fine hotels all over the U.S., Canada and Europe.

FREE DISCOUNT TRAVEL SERVICE

A privileged woman is always jetting to romantic places.

When <u>you</u> fly, just make one phone call for the lowest published airfare at time of booking— <u>or double the difference back!</u>

PLUS—you'll get a $25 voucher to use the first time you book a flight AND <u>5% cash back on every ticket you buy thereafter through the travel service!</u>

PROOF OF PURCHASE

Offer expires October 31, 1996

HP-PP63